1915.

Tales of the Braes of Glenlivet

.

Isobel Grant and others

Compiled by Alasdair Roberts
Illustrated by Ann Dean

Isobel Grant. .

First published in 1999 by
Birlinn Limited
Unit 8 Canongate Venture
Edinburgh EH8 8BH

ISBN 1 84158 08 7

British Library Cataloguing-in-Publication Data
A catalogue record of this book is available from
the British Library

Typeset by Textype, Cambridge
Printed and bound in Great Britain

Contents

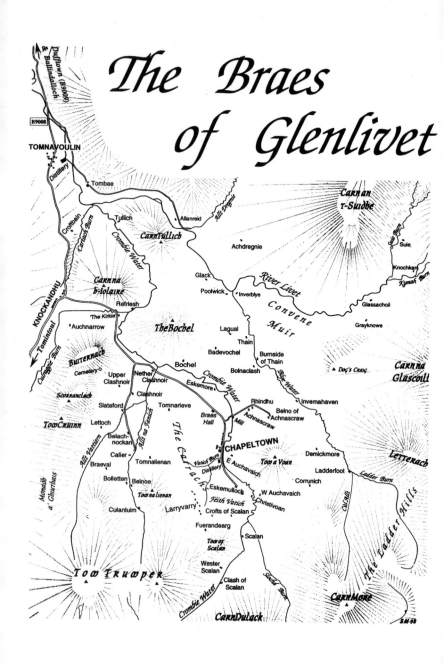

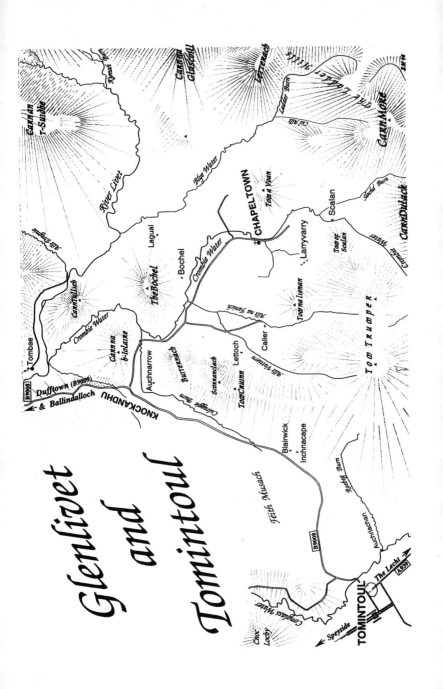

1
·
Welcome to the Braes

·

The Braes of Glenlivet lie beyond Ben Rinnes, on the eastern edge of the Grampian mountains and the southern edge of what is now Moray District. The area used to be in Upper Banffshire. The nearest settlement which anyone outside the area has heard of is Tomintoul, the highest village in the Highlands. The Whisky Trail of the Tourist Board takes in Tomintoul and also the Glenlivet Distillery at Minmore, where the Livet joins the Avon at the lower end of Glenlivet. The Braes district does not include Minmore, although lower Glenlivet was part of its wider world even before the days of motor transport. The hamlet of Tomnavoulin also had a visitor centre but the manufacture of Tamvoulin whisky ceased a while ago. Braes people drive down to the Tomnavoulin shop for papers and petrol and groceries because it is nearer than Tomintoul (and a lot nearer than Elgin with its chain stores and supermarkets).

There is a footbridge across the river from Tomnavoulin to join the Tombae road which goes three miles up the Livet to a car park at Allanreid. This diversion does not lead to the Braes of Glenlivet – certainly not by car – but is worth taking for its pleasantly wooded scenery. The most unexpected feature, along a narrow country road leading nowhere, is a large

Gothic-style church, especially because a neatly painted board proclaims it to be the Roman Catholic Church of the Incarnation, Tombae. It is one of three such chapels in this remarkable corner of Scotland.

Two miles up the Tomintoul road from Tomnavoulin, just after the Pole Inn, there is a side road on the left which leads into the Braes of Glenlivet. It is signposted Chapeltown and Clashnoir. After a few hundred yards the road turns sharp right in front of a house called The Kirkie which represents the Church of Scotland's attempt, in Victorian times, to reform the people of the Braes. Down behind this holiday cottage where Presbyterian sermons were once delivered flows the Crombie burn – the nearest thing to a river in the Braes of Glenlivet. The Bochel hill rears up steeply on the far bank like a sentinel. The name has been traced to *buchaille*, the Gaelic for a herdsman, and it certainly gives the impression of guarding the fold. 'Braes' means the area above, in this case above the Livet, and the river forms a second barrier as it curves round from the Glen of Suie. Families from that remote place of shepherds and gamekeepers used to make their way to Chapeltown for school, shop and church.

Once past the Bochel, fields and pasture open out with the ground rising gently on both sides: the Braes of Glenlivet have been likened to a punch bowl. First on the left stands the Bochel farm, which was Isobel Grant's later childhood home. The road winds on before coming to a fork, where there is a signpost showing right for Clashnoir in the 'back' side of the Braes. Carry on towards Chapeltown. Round the corner a straight road lies ahead through some forestry plantation, then on past the Braes Hall and croft houses close to the road. The last of these, on the right, is Comelybank of Isobel's early childhood. Finally the corbie-stepped tower of Chapeltown's church emerges from a shelter of trees. It announces itself once again as curiously Catholic for rural Scotland, with a white and blue statue of the Blessed Virgin Mary above the door.

This is very nearly the end of the road. To get a true feeling for this world's end of a place, however, carry on past the

Chivas Distillery to the car park at Eskemulloch. Stretch limbs, take deep breaths of pure air, check footwear. A display board prepared by the Glenlivet Estate shows several walks, and a final signpost marked Scalan leads you on to a deeply rutted farm track.

Half a mile further on, concealed till then below a dip in the land, lies the former seminary of Scalan, its freshly-harled gable showing up pale through the trees. Reconstruction work has been in hand. First thoughts for visitors who have consulted the guidebook must be of the school or 'old college' where boys, boarding up to twelve at a time in the 18th century, studied Latin with a view to becoming priests. But further along the track, when Scalan can be seen from the front across a wooden bridge, the impression changes. A notice-board confirms that this is the place, a second sign marks the Bishop's Well, but other structures catch the eye. Two water-wheels suggest an agricultural centre of some importance, and a scattering of buildings make it clear that Scalan was also a farmtown. During the last century it was home to fifty people and several families, as listed by successive government censuses. The 1991 census enumerator found one man and a dog at Scalan.

Tales of the Braes of Glenlivet is not about church history (for that see John Watts' *Scalan,* marking two hundred years since the college closed in 1799), but it is about people who went to church. They gathered at Chapeltown for Sunday Mass, and also for a 'news' afterwards with neighbours they might not have seen for a week. Some went to church more often than others, partly depending on distance. This book recalls 'the Scalan' as a farmtown (and all the others like it), not Scalan the seminary. The same social emphasis is to be found in the 'Brief History of the Braes', added to the end for those who enjoy going further back into the past than living memory.

The greater part of the book consists of the lively living memories of one woman. Isobel Grant is responsible for most of the tales, although Ann Lamb follows on with her own story of childhood. Nurse Lamb, as she is still remembered, grew up at Larryvarry during the opening years of the century. After a varied career in nursing she has herself been in receipt of care at Stonehaven during its closing years. Isobel Grant introduced herself to me at one of the gatherings which bring hundreds of people to Scalan each summer for worship and renewal of old acquaintance; membership of the Scalan Association has risen steadily while restoration has been going on in recent years. Isobel Grant obviously had much to offer from her enthusiastic way of talking, but it was only when letters started to arrive that the special quality of her memories became apparent. Isobel left the Braes during the Depression, but in a lifetime of moves around Scotland and England she has never lost touch. Return visits, letters and phone calls enable this grand old lady, who lives in the heart of London near Oxford Circus, to know what is going on in Glenlivet before some of the residents. And distance has given her a clear memory of what used to go on, seventy years ago and more.

In recent times there has been a remarkable upsurge of interest in roots, and thousands of people support the Family History Society in Aberdeen. This army of amateur genealogists (the largest in Scotland) makes use of parish registers, census records, gravestones and a growing range of printed sources on microfiche – and now the Internet. Isobel Grant adds something to that search for ancestors. She is like everyone's great aunt who used to speak about relations when the world was young – tedious to children, more so to teenagers, yet how often people look back in their mature years and think, 'I wish I'd paid attention – I wish I'd written it down!' But Isobel is more of a chronicler than a compiler of family trees. Her highly personal memories come from her own time or else her mother's, although the arrival at Chapeltown of the young woman who became famous locally as Granny Bochel takes us back to the 1870s. She has a firm grasp of the Grants, Stuarts, McPhersons, Lambs, McHardys and all the rest who made the Braes such a social place in these days. Beyond that, she has the woman of the tribe's amazing knowledge of where they all went!

These names and relations would have as little interest as someone else's family tree if it were not for the fact that they are all mixed in with her stories. Isobel has an instinctive sense of what makes a good story – often quite a short story, more of a tale. Since most of them come from her childhood, there is a freshness about them which appeals. Equally, however, Isobel has been able to follow many of her characters through lives which are often remarkably long. As an octogenarian herself, she speaks on behalf of old people everywhere. Isobel's material came through the letter-box of the Braes Chapel-house when my wife Deirdre and I were tenants there. Deirdre's labour of love on the word-processor made it possible to edit dozens of hand-written letters about obscure people and places until complicated relationships became clear.

Part of my task was to consult maps and walk the ground – rather slowly, as one who avoids the barren mountain top and welcomes signs of former habitation. This book is for anyone who ever gazed on a ruined building and wondered who lived there. Ann Dean's 'Crofts of Scalan', linked to the Larryvarry of Ann Lamb, evokes the sadness of a deserted land with old people left behind and young ones forced elsewhere for a living, but there is nothing sad about Isobel Grant's tales. Ann's drawings catch both moods by turn. These glimpses of past time provide a vivid sense of life in the old Scots countryside, but this is no everyday (yesterday) story of country folk. There is a pride of locality among Braes people, once described by the folklorist Hamish Henderson as 'the real Scots'.

Partly because of the loss of people which began before Ann Lamb's time and gathered speed in Isobel Grant's, this is an area of good walks which are remarkably unspoiled by modern standards. The Ladder Hills have no Munros or peaks, and few walkers now come over the Ladder Trail from Strathdon. In contrast to over-used tracks like the Pennine Way, up to a hundred metres across, the Whisky Road, which smugglers took past Scalan, is lost in the heather and cries out to be tramped into place again. There is a wide choice of routes for Tomintoul and Glenlivet in Sir Edward Peck's *Avonside Explored*, and the Glenlivet Estate has produced an audio-cassette of nine guided drives. Victor Gaffney's *Tomintoul: its Glens and its People* is very informative on the history of the same wide area. Priscilla Gordon-Duff has compiled a local booklet out of talks with Braes people – Bill and Irene Grant of Nether Clashnoir, Sandy Matheson of the Scalan, and Jessie Robb, who was the oldest resident when she died in 1995. Mrs Gordon-Duff's emphasis on what the Braes of Glenlivet have to offer the city-dweller is caught in her title: *Water of Life – and a Breath of Fresh Air.*

In 1946 an incomer to the Braes wrote in the *Banffshire Journal*, 'Our postman informs me that when he first started on his rounds in this district some forty years ago, he had to pay visits to fifty-two houses the walls of which, in many cases, are not even standing today. Again, he tells me that down from Scalan when he was a schoolboy trooped thirty-two children to Chapeltown School – now two alone walk that road.' This rural postman, James Lamb of Tomnareave, was better placed than any census officer when it came to knowing who lived where. A colleague of these days, Postie Grant of Tomnavoulin, was captured in verse on the neighbouring round:

> Up and doon the Livet side he weathered mony a gale.
> 'Gainst the Kyma's eastern blast he somehow did prevail.
> He struggled up the Corrie Burn in spate, in slush an' sna',
> But when it cam' a bonny day he seen forgot it a'.

James Grant had connections at the head of the Braes of Glenlivet, as he was married to a sister of John and Maggie Sharp who lived (according to Isobel Grant's precise recollection) 'at the house opposite the Drovers'. He was a man of letters in more than one sense, as shown by the following *Journal* report.

The Year in the Uplands

The year opened in bright, fresh weather and continued pretty much like that throughout the entire winter and spring. It was, however, a particularly cold period with frequent gales, but there was very little frost or snow. Indeed only on one or two occasions was it necessary to traverse the roads with snow ploughs. May was a passable month and June days, as it happened, gave us our only summer. On the 16th of the month the upper areas of the country suffered a very severe thunderstorm, July contributed rain almost daily, and August did no better except for one week at the commencement of the month. Later the rains laid and twisted many grand oat crops.

Harvesting commenced in September and continued far into October. Although the bulk of the crops in the area has now been got to the stackyard somehow, there are still here and there many acres of battered crops to be cut. The lack of sunshine and abnormal rainfall will undoubtedly seriously reduce the quantity and quality of oats this year. Much of the straw is likely to be greatly inferior to that of normal years. Potatoes, too, especially those grown on flat or wet lands, are disappointing. In other respects, however, agriculturists have come out well. Despite the trail of rain it was amazing how cattle and sheep matured. Of course grass was in abundance everywhere and still shows much promise. For many years business at the various stock sales had been on the upgrade and this season the tendency in that direction was more in evidence than ever.

Frequent reference has been made to the depopulation of glen places, and events in this year of 1957 clearly showed that the tendency steadily grows. For years, as families moved from the district, children attending the local schools faded gradually in number, and latterly to such an extent that the Education Authority could do no other than close both Tombae and Tomnavoulin Schools. The remaining handful of children are now being conveyed daily by bus to Tomintoul. It is rather a depressing picture for those of an earlier generation to see old institutions of learning now on the scrap heap, but there it is. They served their day and now pass away, for there is little on this earth that can claim to be everlasting.

Depopulation is causing concern in another direction. Postal officials from Ballindalloch upward to Tomintoul have been going of late over the various postal rounds on motor vehicles, presumably to amend existing arrangements. In many places we find today only a handful of houses, with perhaps one or two occupants, a striking contrast to the much more populated conditions prevalent in earlier years, but there still remain occupied homesteads standing here and there on the lone hillsides and to cover these and to give a satisfactory service all over provides something of a problem for the powers concerned.

In view of all this upheaval it may be considered that life in glen places gets gradually more isolated and lonely. To some extent that is true, but every little helps and shortly, we gather, conditions will brighten somewhat when the public library again functions in the area. This boon and blessing to many appeared to have gone when the library departed with the closing of the schools, and so, although we live in a world of troubles and not the least of them the continual upward trend of living costs, we still feel that, to quote Burns, 'We hae aye been provided for and so will we yet.'

J. A. Grant

With these stoic words the old postman, himself a product of rural schools and libraries, laid down his pen. For some years, however, reports of upland weather (and crops and stock and wildlife) had been written with no less eloquence by Robbie Lamb of Fuerandearg, a small farm at the head of the Braes. He contributed fiction and poetry too, as well as the occasional letter. One of these, signed 'Whisky Galore', is clearly his: 'In the recent severe storm we were cut off for weeks until the Dufftown snowplough opened the one and only road. Never once did we hear a complaint. All found their way through the deep snowdrifts to the local grocer who, with a well-stocked store, supplied all their needs and met all their demands with a smile. Truly this hardy race have lived up to the old saying: "The Braes of Glenlivet folk never cry out – until the whisky is done."'

Robbie Lamb's *Journal* duties included the writing of

obituaries for his neighbours, and Robbie's own epitaph was penned by Mairi Gordon who had known him since schooldays: 'All his life he took a lively interest in current affairs and in politics. A great reader, a great speaker, with a sensitive nature and a brilliant mind, he was always in demand for his forthright conversation and dramatic delivery. Robert Lamb was a great patriot, intensely interested in his native land, in the majesty of its hills and the smiling beauty of its valleys. He was interested, too, in the Scottish language and also in the Gaelic names of farms and places. Frequently he sent out verbal appeals and letters to the press begging that the "glens be not denuded of their most precious possession – people".'

Stuart Mitchell's account of the Gaelic names of farms and places which appears towards the end of this book would have satisfied even the exacting standards of Robbie Lamb. Stuart provides a location map to guide the reader and an area map to accompany his place-names. Both are very different from the imaginative frontispiece (planned as the 'Milly-Molly-Mandy map', for anyone who remembers that childhood favourite) which Ann Dean has devised to show Chapeltown's Church, School, Shop and neighbours. Mairi Gordon, who was the last teacher at the Braes school, did great service in making a collection of Robbie Lamb's cuttings (duly preserved by Lindy Shaw) along with other items from the local press. In yellowing newsprint there is lively writing aplenty to support the tales of Isobel Grant. Much of it presents the activities of the area from a masculine point of view, providing useful balance to girlish recollections, but the spirit of the Braes is certainly there in the memories of Isobel Grant. Despite the book's varied contents and the affectionate editing of the undersigned, she remains the principal author.

Alasdair Roberts

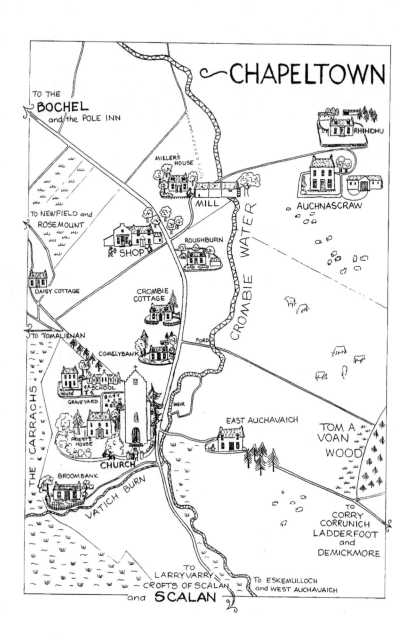

2

·

Beginnings

·

My mother Elspeth Ann Stuart grew up at Christivoan, a house which used to be opposite Auchavaich, with her granny and grandfather and her aunt Isa Stuart, who was only ten years older. Later she became Isa Stuart Westerton. There was another aunt, Jane Ann Stuart Tomnareave. She worked as a cook in Edinburgh before coming back to the Braes to marry. When Elsie, my mother, was fourteen the family moved to Comelybank, beside the church. Her uncle Charles Stuart was the local cobbler, Charlie Shoemaker – his little shop is still there. He made all the men's boots, and mother never had a corn. My Stuart great-grandparents both lived to the age of ninety and then one died on the other's funeral day. I am called Isabella after my great-grandmother Isabella Stuart, who was married to a shepherd. I was two years old when she died.

I was born in 'blin' drift' at 6 a.m. on 26th March, 1915. Dr Black Tomintoul couldn't get there through the snow, so Nurse Lamb's mother acted as midwife. If we met on the road in years to come Mrs Lamb always said, 'You are one of my babies!' and sometimes gave me sixpence. The Tomintoul doctor did the Braes in those days, not the Glenlivet one. When one new doctor arrived in Glenlivet he visited all the houses and said, 'No need for me here. Every house has a kale yaird.' He thought there would be no need for his medicines. We survived, but it was survival of the fittest. It's sad to read on the gravestones how so many died young.

My father William Gordon Grant was from Lagual on Blyeside. He came home to marry from Canada, where he had been working for seven years building railways. Then he died on the Feast of Our Lady of Mount Carmel, 16th July, 1914, so I was a 'posthumous baby' – that's the name given if the father has died before the date of birth on the registered birth certificate. My oldest sister Mary was one year eight months when he died and my other sister Margaret was seven months. Father insisted that both of his first two daughters had the middle name Gordon after his mother Jessie Gordon Lagual. Mam found herself a widow with three daughters – Mary, Meggie and me.

She walked down to Tomnavoulin to register the birth. It had to be done before three weeks were up, and she left it till the last day to get her strength back for the seven-mile walk there and back. She never liked the name she was given herself, Elspeth – she said Elsie wasn't a saint's name. At that time you wouldn't ask the priest to baptise your baby without a saint's name. I said, 'Well you could be the first St Elsie.' She certainly deserved it.

My godmother was Lena Stuart of Roughburn, across from the Shop, who went on to become a teacher at the Queen's Cross convent school in Aberdeen. She was only ten years old. Elsie McPherson stood by her at the christening and carried me because Lena was so young. Elsie lived at Corrunich. Father Wiseman did the baptism. Of course my mother was still at home resting after the birth. I was supposed to be called Helena, after Lena, but they forgot to ask the name before leaving for Church. They had heard Isabella mentioned, after my great-grandmother who was living with us at Comelybank, so they just called me that.

There were no large christenings in those days or any parties afterwards. The mother always stayed in bed for ten days till she was fully recovered, then was back at work within the fortnight. They used to have a small sponge cake that cost about one and sixpence (not iced) for the godmother on the table and there was a cup of tea. Lena's father Charles Stuart was my mother's half-brother, the oldest of the first family – there were nine of them.

Widow's pensions didn't come in until 1916. Before that they got nothing from the government, although the Priest gave all widows one pound at Christmas. I think old age pensions started in 1912. They got ten shillings a week and were delighted with it. Men could buy black twist tobacco for their pipes which lasted a week, and the women bought groceries – a whole basketful. Of course Children's Allowance is a more recent thing, invented by Mussolini.

Wives had to wait till the husband was seventy before any pension came into the house. In later years a welfare officer came round and asked in every house if they were managing. Of course they didn't go in for luxurious furniture and everything to match so he thought they must be very poor. All said they were managing fine. Mam was thrilled when her new pension book had an extra thirteen shillings. But one woman had a farm and two sons to support her, and when her husband's will went in the paper they took the extra money back. Another woman retired early and went on the insurance.

The inspector came round, and when he discovered she kept six hens he took sixpence a week off. It never occurred to him that she had to buy food for the hens. She kept a goat for milk, but had the sense to tether it out of sight.

We had a wonderful cow at Comelybank which gave three pails of milk every day. Of course on the croft, being small, we could put on more manure and get better grass as well as fine crops of corn, swede turnips and potatoes. The crofters used to take their cows along the sides of the roads to eat the grass. Now it has to wait till the Council comes to cut it. Grand-uncle Charlie Stuart was a great gardener. There was a berry garden at the back as well as a vegetable garden, and we kept hens.

Mam did whatever jobs were available. She cleaned the Church and the School, and did washing for her brother's wife who had the Shop-house. Mrs Grant Riv helped her and they both got five shillings for the day's washing. Like all the others, of course, she worked in the fields at harvest time. We had very good neighbours and relatives in the Braes, and we were handed down clothes from Lena and Agnes at the Shop-house, who were older. We wanted for nothing.

The trees along the road in front of the Chapeltown council houses were all planted by my Uncle Charles Stuart who had the Shop. I was so glad the Council didn't remove them when the houses went up in the 1960s. His copper beech trees are still in the front garden of Comelybank, and the lilac and honeysuckle are there as well. The aspen tree remains at Crombie Cottage next door, just inside the fence. As a child I found it fascinating to watch the leaves quiver all the time.

The boys played football on a flat piece of wasteland across the Crombie burn, and my sisters and I used to watch from our bay bedroom window upstairs on the light nights. It was really funny sometimes when the ball landed in the burn and they had to run down the edge to retrieve it. Granny didn't let them play football on a Sunday. She liked it to be a peaceful day and would tell them to go for a walk up the hill.

Alistair Stuart Easterton trained there as a boy and went on to compete in Highland Games all over Scotland. He was one of a family of nine, but his mother fed him on bacon and eggs to help him to get energy. He became the greatest light-weight athlete, and we even saw him throwing the hammer on Pathé News at the cinema. Alistair was offered training as a boxer but refused. I expect he didn't want his nose flattened to spoil his good looks. The Stuarts left the district, but when Alastair worked for a poultry firm he came back round the farms selling hen food. We had a huge double-yolked egg when he was there once, so we told him, 'This is the kind of eggs we always get since using your hen food.' We thought of him as a city gent then, because he wore grey spats and a smart suit.

> Before the war Alistair Stuart, the 'pocket Hercules', was un-rivalled as a Scots style thrower of the 16lb hammer. In 1934 he set up a record at the Aboyne Games of 125 ft 7 which stood for thirty years. He had developed a rapid swing which enabled him to outdistance taller competitors. Mr Stuart and his wife later ran the Ashvale fish restaurant in Aberdeen.

When I was very small I started knitting – I must have been about four years old. I was knitting a pair of garters for my Granny. She was rather stout, and as I was getting tired of knitting I kept measuring her leg. It needed to go round three times and tied in a bow. I remember being so proud when I finished my first sock.

At one time there were only foot bridges over the Crombie – horses and carts went through wherever there was a ford. In the 1920s large bridges strong enough to take cars and lorries were built at the Bochel, the Mill, Easterton, Auchavaich and Scalan – also at Vatich where the Distillery is now. We used to wade under the bridge there as children.

There was a large stone slab covering the water where it was diverted in front of Cromby Cottage. It went all the way down to the Mill to turn the wheel. Jeems (that's James Stuart who stayed next door at Crombie Cottage) used to lift the slab and fill pails of water for the cows to drink. One night I was staying

the night with Mary as her father was away. She was saying her prayers by the bedroom window as usual when she noticed a tramp going along the road to Auchavaich barn. We laughed to see him pick up the cows' pail and drink from it.

Anne Turner came from Dufftown – she was an aunt to my six Turner nieces on their father's side. Annie married our next-door neighbour Johnnie Stuart at Crombie Cottage when the bride and groom were both aged fifty. Johnnie wanted to marry her years before but she stayed at home to help her mother. They had fifteen years together. As a boy, Johnnie used to come to our house at Comelybank where he was able to make as much noise as he liked, because his father had to have silence for his newspaper. He was like a brother. With his first wages Johnnie bought us all toys at Christmas. He was training to be a banker, but hated it and left to be a shepherd.

The Orphan 'mang the Heather

The frigid eastern wind blew strong, the sleety snow did batter,
The tempest-laden leaden sky the Easter sun did smother.
On Larrievarrie's windswept muir, where deer and hares foregather,
He shivered in the angry blast – the orphan 'mang the heather.

His birth no smiling morn did greet, no mother's fond caressing,
Dame Nature in her cruel mood on him bestowed no blessing.
His trembling legs, his drooping ears ice-crusted snow did fetter.
Anon, he gave a piteous bleat – the orphan 'mang the heather.

Now cosy in the shepherd's plaid beside a blazing ingle,
Wi' jest a wee drap Usquebaugh to make his heart strings tingle,
With luck some day he'll be a tup or else a handsome wether,
Tough member of the Blackfaced breed – the orphan 'mang the heather.

Rob Uan

We often got a late snowfall in April, after the lambing had begun. We would bring a lamb in frozen stiff but then it revived – usually in a basket with a blanket in front of the fire. I once tried to revive one with whisky but I should have diluted it. The lamb just gave a gasp and passed out. Most of the men were shepherds during the winter in these days. They came home to do other work in summer when the lambs were all born and the sheep were grazing safely in the fields.

There were so many Stuarts and Grants in the Braes that you were always called by your farm or else a by-name. At Comely-bank the three of us sisters were always called Mary of Bell's, Meggie of Bell's and Baby of Bell's, Bell being my great-grandmother's name. She was a Cameron who came from a house above Auchnarrow called Starryhillock. A woman called Margaret Grant came back from America so we called her Miss Grant California. She hadn't written home for thirty years and thought her brother might be still alive, but he died young. My granny at Comelybank met her on the road and asked her to come and stay with us for a while – she had to get Charlie Shoemaker to agree because it was his house. Miss Grant was tall and very beautiful, and she used to say to Mam, 'You should put powder on your face, Elsie. It's very beneficial to the skin.' Mam just smiled. She never needed make-up. She had that lovely skin that goes with auburn hair. Anyhow nobody in Glenlivet wore make-up then – they couldn't afford beauty aids.

Miss Grant was fussy and didn't like the way we used two uncovered pails of water in the scullery, so Meggie had to fill a large whisky bottle for her from the pump. She got a penny a day for that. Miss Grant also gave the first one of us three who was in bed a penny. I expect she wanted peace in the evening. It was always Mary or me who won it because Meggie folded her clothes. Miss Grant California got Mam to go with her over to Invernahaven. She took off her shoes and stockings and paddled in all the pools in the heather as she had done in childhood. After a while she went to relatives in Elgin, and the last we heard of her was a card from London. Mam thought she was in the Secret Service.

3

·

Connections

·

My Grant grandfather left the Braes like so many other young men at that time. He sailed to Canada from Glasgow hoping to make a home out there for his wife Jessie Gordon and their four children, Margaret, Alex, Adam and William. My father William, the youngest, was born in 1886. But Jessie didn't want to go to Canada after her husband. Maybe she was ill, because soon after that she died. That was when the children went to Lagual. Then he wrote asking Mary, her sister, to come out with them, but she didn't want to go either. Mary Gordon never married, and in later life she lived alone at the Glack. She was deaf and had a huge ear trumpet, but Mairi and Lucy gave her all the news of the Braes. I remember her well. Robbie Lamb wrote her obituary:

> Miss Mary Gordon was a native of the Braes of Glenlivet, being born at Lagual 84 years ago. In her youth she was an expert in dressmaking, and her services in that respect were much in request by the womenfolk of that period. Apart from a serious defect in her hearing, Miss Gordon enjoyed robust health until some months ago. All her life she was a great reader – indeed for many years most of her time was given over to books and to letter writing. Though

living on the lone hillside far away from many con-
veniences, this grand old lady was never lonely, for she
loved her home and adored in summer and winter the
majesty of the surrounding hills, the bonny birken woods,
and the gleam of the Livet river flowing gently down the
glen. In her home Miss Gordon was hospitality in every
sense of the word, and on occasions when neighbours
gathered round her fireside such meetings were ever of a
truly Highland welcome.

The 1891 census shows four children aged from five to twelve
being looked after at Lagual by Mary Gordon. Her mother Mrs
Margaret Gordon, the children's granny, was a widow by then
and the man of the house was William, aged thirty-four. He
wrote poems for national papers, and one of them paid this
tribute to him:

> Mr W. F. Gordon is a Highlander, having been born in the
> Braes o' Glenlivet where he still resides. He is a farmer,
> and woos the muse amidst the dark hills and green glens
> of the north. Mr Gordon has written a great deal of verse,
> being a frequent contributor to the newspapers and
> periodicals of the day. He is also a musician, and can play
> both the bagpipes and the violin, particularly the former,
> of which he is extremely fond. He has won numerous
> prizes for bagpipe-playing, and at more than one
> Highland gathering has carried off the prize for the best-
> dressed Highlander.

In 1897 Willie married Agnes Stuart the Mill, who was only
nineteen, and brought her to live at Lagual. That was when
Mary Gordon moved out to a house between Badevochel and
Westview which is gone now. She brought the four children up
there herself and never married. Her brother-in-law sent home
the fares but Mary used the money to bring them up, and after
a while his letters stopped. When my father William went out
to Canada at the age of nineteen and worked on building the
railway, he tried to trace his father by advertising in the papers

but got no answer. He came home and married my mother in 1912. His brother Alex Grant had a great reputation as a wrestler in Glasgow. He married a woman from Ladybank and went out to take a croft at Rockhampton in Queensland. They had a boy and a girl – we heard that both mother and daughter were afraid of cows, not being used to country life! A Grant cousin from Glasgow visited the daughter on a world tour, and she wrote and asked me to go out and visit her.

There were more than twenty years between Willie Gordon Lagual and his wife. They had ten children, but several died young. The Laguals were all very intelligent and Willie Gordon himself was brilliant. He died when Lucy the youngest was three, and their mother was left to bring them up on her own. Louis became a great piper like his father. I remember him well, and he still writes home from New Zealand. He worked at Belno of Achnascraw before going out there in the 1920s, first to Australia as a shepherd and then to the sheep-shearing. Electric shears started there long before they reached Britain. When Robert McHardy Calier was seven years old he met a lady out walking. She asked if he was going to the shearing and he said, 'The clippin', you mean.'

A Clipping

Though only a boy, I took part in the day's proceedings. I can remember well how, with beating heart, I stealthily drew near the gate to the fold, and having entered would select one of the flock within. Then began a performance which, when I think of it now, must have been funny in the extreme. Round and round we would go, my tiny feet in full pursuit until, aided and spurred on by shouts of encouragement from the onlookers, I would finally grasp one horn and wrestle with all the strength in my puny arms. They were big and strong, these Highland sheep of the blackfaced breed, and more often than not the struggle went against me, but how proud I was when I managed to drag my unwilling victim out to the green grass and the unwelcome attention of the shearers.

In the afternoon there would be tea, with scones and fresh butter, and I would lie on the grass looking up at the sun and listen to a lark away up there carolling a melody which could only have been composed by the Great Being in the Paradise Beyond. Yes, these were happy days, and on these occasions part of my joy embraced a visit to the shop for beer. It always used to be Whitbreads, in very large bottles, and many a smile and beckoning look was flashed upon me as I toiled up the brae and over the knowe.

At last all would be over. The sheep, shorn and so much smaller than they had seemed to be before, would be turned again to the hills, and over the summit of the distant Slochs a gentle creeping mist would silently appear. Lassie, her wise head between her toes and her brown eyes quietly brooding, would look up at me and flap her tail as though in mute appreciation of a day's work well done. With a chorus of 'guidnichts', all the helpers would depart across the little grassy bridge and far away beneath the crags a solitary ewe would bleat in mournful response. Entering the kitchen, I would walk over to the dresser and, lifting a china hen which was my own special property, I would deposit beneath her the many silvery coins which had been slipped in my pockets that afternoon.

James Grant

Louis Gordon Lagual met Nurse Lamb's brother John over in New Zealand when he was living in bothies, but John couldn't stand the rough life there and came back to this country. It was in the days when you were given a bit of land free and cut down the forest yourself in order to get a farm started. Louis came home for a break after thirty years when his sister Mairi was teaching in the Braes school. She went there from a post in Aberdeen to take her mother into the Chapeltown School-house, as she was getting frail. Louis looked after the mother during the day when Mairi was teaching. She lived for six weeks after he came home. When it was nice weather and Mairi was in school, her mother would sometimes walk off to Lagual. Her sons watched her till she got out of sight below the Shop, then went home, but they didn't let her see they were following.

Lucy Gordon used to stay at Roughburn when she taught at the Braes school. She married Bill Shaw, who first came to Glenlivet for the fishing. He liked the Blye burn. Their daughter now lives in Oban – my cousin Lindy, who has three very clever daughters. That comes from the Laguals. She had a letter from her Uncle Louis to say that his wife had died in New Zealand (he married late in life) so she wrote back asking him to come over for a holiday. She wondered if he would know anyone who grew up with him. John Grant from Achnascraw died at Perth in his nineties. Louie, who grew up at Tomnareave, is still in Keith. Louis and John Grant share a birthday, as the sisters Isa and Jane Ann both had their babies on the same day.

Meg Grant, who now lives at Tomnavoulin, married Charlie Grant Westerton. That was a farm nearby, but the house has been done up and there's a pool in the garden. His childhood was spent at Achnascraw, and she was boarded out from Edinburgh to live at Broombank above the Church. The McGillivrays moved into Achnascraw when the Grants went to Westerton. Charlie had a bad heart in later years, and he sat by the fireside a lot telling Meg all about the Braes and how each family was related. Many a holiday we spent at Westerton as children. We played whist every night – that family were experts and won prizes at all the whist drives, and they taught us how to play. When the Braes Hall was built in 1930, down the road from Chapeltown, we had good whist drives and invited Tomintoul members over. Tea and sandwiches were provided, and then the Braes players would be invited over there. There were lots of social occasions before the war. Dances in wartime had to be in aid of Red Cross Funds, and petrol was allowed for a bus to Tomintoul and back. Concerts gave people a chance to perform and they started up again at the end of the war.

> At the concert and dance in aid of the Welcome Home Fund, held in the Braes Hall, Father MacWilliam presided. The artistes were mostly local, each item being greeted by rounds of applause from a large and appreciative audience. Miss Nicol, Schoolhouse, tastefully rendered the accompaniments. Those who took part in the programme were:– Jas. Stuart, Alex. Grant,

W. and C. Grant, Pte. Walsh, R. Lamb, Mrs Joiner, and Nurse
Matheson. The arrangements were carried out by Messrs. J.
Stuart and W. Grant. As a result of their efforts the fund will
benefit by a substantial sum. An enjoyable dance followed to
music by the Strathdown Band. Mr W. Rattray was MC.

Father Donald Grant was a relation of mine who died while
still quite young. His Aunt Teresa was the youngest of thirteen
Grant children. She was named after St Teresa of Lisieux, and
Donald was born on her feast day, 3rd October, 1948. Their
mother was my grandmother's sister at Christivoan. They were
all born at Achnascraw before the move to Westerton and then
Tomnavoulin farm. My grand-aunt, Isa Stuart Westerton, was
Father Donald's grandmother. He was a Carmelite priest in the
Aberdeen University chaplaincy, but often went up to stay in a
cottage above Tomnavoulin, especially when he was recovering
from chemotherapy. He used to come and see me in London
and ask questions for the family tree which he was putting on
his computer. Father Donald grew up in Perth but always loved
Glenlivet.

We lived at Comelybank for ten years until Mam married
George Grant and moved to the Bochel. Jean and Charlie are
the surviving children of the second marriage, although there
was also a baby, George Allan, who died at ten months. My
stepfather was known as Piper Grant in the war when he served
in the Gordon Highlanders. He got shrapnel in his knee and
was a cripple the rest of his life. It couldn't have been much
fun leading the men into battle playing the bagpipes, and I
believe they stopped it after a while. My sister Jean has his
photo and medals framed in her house at Forgue.

On June 14 1965 in Stephen's Hospital, Dufftown, the death
occurred of Mr George Grant, Bochel, Braes of Glenlivet, aged
83. A piper in the fighting sixth territorial battalion of the
Gordon Highlanders, he was early in France in 1914 and was
wounded at Neuve Chapelle. Unfit for more active service, he
was discharged and returned to the Braes where he farmed
Bochel for a number of years, the tenancy now being held by

his son Charlie. Both piper and fiddler, he was for long in great request at weddings and for all classes of entertainments. He could sing a comic song or tell a good story and he was also possessed of natural wit. Some of his sayings are still in use. A splendid planner of farm work, he was not slow to give his practical advice and assistance to others.

His mother, Granny Bochel, came from Aberchirder to Chapeltown in 1874 when she was twenty to help the house-keeper to the new priest, Father MacEachron. She married two years later. She used to recite a poem about 'the Reverend Glennie, a priest of fame, God bless for aye his honoured name. He refused to rest or stay at hame but went to the hills in the morning.' That was the priest who had been nearly thirty years at Chapeltown and left as she arrived. It's from a poem called 'The Lass o' the Lecht' about a girl who got lost and died in the snow. They didn't find her till spring, although hundreds of men went out searching.

Granny Bochel stayed with us. One time she went to Portsoy for a holiday, to relatives on the Moray Firth, and that left our mother plenty of work to do on the farm. Granny was away a fortnight, so a few days before her return Mam rushed a letter away to her in case she thought she was being neglected. She used to write letters between 11 p.m. and midnight, and being tired wrote the address as 'Mrs Grant, Rosehall, Port Said' – but no Banffshire. The boy that posted it at the Shop on his way to school never looked at the address. When Granny came back she was quite upset about not getting a letter or postcard but Mam said, 'I did write.' Three months later, the letter arrived back from Port Said in Egypt – it had gone all the way there and back for a penny-ha'penny stamp! I suppose they realised out there when they saw the postmark was Scotland, tried perhaps Port Gordon, then Portsoy. Granny had to laugh that her letter had gone round the world. She took an interest in everything that was going on.

From Tomnavoulin, Knockandhu and Tomintoul the friends of the Chapeltown Dramatic Society came to the Braes on April 2

1948 to see their production of Andrew P. Wilson's rollicking comedy 'The Bogey Man'. Some may have had doubts before the play, but the confident and sure characterisation, the high standard of the acting, the correct timing and perfect team-work made doubt give way to a pleasant surprise that they could do so well in the Braes. Among those who witnessed with joy this singular triumph was the nonagenarian Mrs Grant of Bochel. Mr Coutts delighted the audience with selections during the interval, and a splendid evening was rounded off with dancing to Mr Ross's Band. The cast was:- Annie Dobbie, Miss E. Hornby; Janet Purdie, Mrs A. Turner; Maggie Michie, Miss M. Clarke; Lizzie Stuart, Miss D. Stuart; Willie Michie, Mr Wm. Grant; Tom Purdie, Mr. R. Grant; Mattha Purdie, Mr Charles Grant; Peter Leerie, Mr E. Hornby; Jimmie Lowrie, Mr C. McGillivray; Snecky Tamson, Mr J. Healey.

The wives used to knit their husbands' socks and gloves, and one even made shirts on the sewing machine. Wives also knitted vests and long drawers for their husbands in special pale pink wool. Mam and Dad preferred grey flannel next to the skin, but Granny Bochel wore a calico vest summer and winter. She used to tell the doctor that if she got a cold she cured it with water, not his medicine – she called it the water of life. My cousin Lindy, a clever girl at school, once said to Granny, 'You must have lived in Queen Victoria's reign.' Of course Granny was well into middle age by the end of the reign. She had a lovely picture of Queen Victoria sitting in a chair in her old age, all dressed in black with a mutch on her head – quite like Granny Bochel.

Grand Old Lady of the Glen

Two summers ago, in 1951, I was camping on the banks of the Crombie burn at the foot of the hill in Glenlivet called the Bochel (writes Helen Fisher). That is how I came to know the grand old lady of the glen, Mrs Annie Grant. Everyone in the Braes of Glenlivet knows her as Granny Bochel after the hill farm where she lives with her son and daughter-in-law. In spite of all family suggestions to 'take it easy', she insists on doing all manner of chores about the house and the farm. Her mind is sharp and clear, and she has a keen sense of humour.

When I was there Granny Bochel met with an alarming accident. She fell while doing a bit of gardening and her brow was badly lacerated. It was a serious mishap for a woman of ninety-eight but she picked herself up and, to the great alarm of the household, came indoors with blood streaming down her face. With some difficulty she was persuaded to go to bed to await the doctor. He decided she needed hospital attention. Badly shaken though she was, the indomitable old lady walked unassisted from the house to the ambulance. After a spell in hospital at Elgin, where she was a favourite of the nurses, she returned home none the worse for her experience. And she still does her bit of gardening.

Centenarian Throws a Party

It was a great day in the Braes of Glenlivet yesterday when Mrs Anne Grant of the Bochel gave a party on her hundredth birthday – 17th August, 1953. Last week she had this notice posted up in the local shop at Chapeltown: 'Granny Bochel hopes to see all her friends at the hall at four o'clock on Monday, 17th August, 1953, to celebrate her hundredth birthday. There will be songs, recitations and Highland dancing. No gifts, by request.'

And her friends came, between three and four hundred of them, in specially-chartered buses from Dufftown and Buckie, in cars and shooting brakes, on bicycle and on foot. After the dinner dishes were washed there was no more work done in the glen yesterday. Sunday suits and white collars and party frocks were donned, and by four o'clock the grassy frontage to the little village hall was like a corner of the Epsom downs on Derby Day! In the guests crowded until the hall was packed, and at the top sat Granny ready to receive them, a bowl of a hundred flowers and a cake with a hundred candles on the table in front of her. She wore a violet woollen cape – a birthday present – over her black frock, held a posy of roses, and with her legs crossed she sat back and chatted to those who had come to pay court to such a wonderful old lady.

Meanwhile the little post office at the Shop was becoming so inundated with telegrams and cables – over a hundred of them, and after delivering over seventy cards to the Bochel – that the staff had to lock themselves in at one point and, ignoring the people knocking on the door for groceries, work steadily at the telephone. There was a telegram from the Queen. There was a cable from the Pope. There were telegrams from Members of Parliament, from the Catholic Bishop of Aberdeen, from friends and relatives everywhere and, despite all the work, one from the staff of the Chapeltown Post Office. When she heard the Queen's telegram read out Granny Bochel said, 'From the Queen! That was awfu' kind o' her.'

At the party were most of her sixty-three descendants, to the fifth generation. After Father Phillips had congratulated Granny publicly on everyone's behalf it was thought that all the excitement would be too much for Granny to make her own reply, and her oldest son, Mr George Grant, got up to speak for her. But halfway through he was interrupted by Granny getting on to her feet and doing her own talking, thanking everybody charmingly for coming to her party: 'I hope you will all have as happy a life as I have had,' she said. 'She's kicking me oot,' said her son, himself nearly eighty, when he could get a word in again, 'But I'll finish my speech in spite o' her!'

Then the cake candles were lit, and Granny blew out most of them by herself. Tea was served and a concert followed. A group of little girls sang and did Highland dances, and there were three original compositions written in honour of the great occasion – a poem by a nephew, Mr William Farquharson, another by a friend in Dufftown, and a song by a bard from Skye, Mr Macdonald, which he sang to his own accompaniment.

So great was the company that extra sandwiches had to be cut in the little back room and extra pails of water for tea fetched from the house in the next field. When it was growing dusk in the little hall and the lamps were being lit, Granny thought it was time to go home and leave the young folk to their night of dancing. She was taken by car to her farm up the hill across the Crombie . . . happy, calm, and, confessing it at last, 'kind o' tired'.

Granny Bochel Irons Her Clothes on Her 101st Birthday

How does it feel to be a hundred and one? Granny Bochel says it is better than being a hundred because you can enjoy yourself in your ain hoose without having to go all the way down to the local hall. After breakfast, it being Tuesday, she decided as ever to do her ironing, having washed on Monday – she always does the linen off her own bed and her own clothes, her 'body clothes' as she says. But her daughter-in-law Mrs Elsie Grant put her foot down there.

Granny, who still prefers the old box iron, had just got the stone into the lough of the coal fire in her own room and had the ironing sheet spread out on her little table when her daughter-in-law came into the room and put a stop to her domesticity: 'This is your birthday, Granny, and you'll be having visitors, so you'll have to put the ironing away until tomorrow.' But Granny won in the end. She likes ironing and likes having her picture taken, so later when the press photographer arrived she got out the box iron.

A few minutes after nine o'clock the visitors began to arrive in spite of Granny's resolution to have a quiet day with 'nae fuss'. First to come were relatives from Dundee, then from Tomintoul and Dufftown, and so it went on throughout the day. The family doctor, Dr Paul, came with a bottle of sherry. District Nurse Matheson came with a head of grey wool, which Granny says she will soon knit up into socks 'to keep me oot o' mischief'. Father Phillips came to wish her many happy returns. The same as last year, the post office had to lock its doors – there were over eighty birthday cards, which it took Granny's son and his wife one hour to open and read out. Then one guest arrived from Premnay with the cake – white with pink decorations and a solitary candle to start Granny off on her 'second lap' – she has decided to start counting the years 'a' ower again'.

Outside, while posing among the roses, she told how the garden was all heather and bog when she came to the Bochel as a young bride. She was a hardy young woman, ambitious and hard-working, and often she went out in the fields with the horses and the harrow. When she was widowed her eldest son James was eighteen and she ran the whole farm. Now that task is handed down to her grandson. There were more than a score of people in the kitchen by now, including five little great-granddaughters from Edinburgh, and while the grown-ups got a glass of wine and a slice of cake The Highland Fling was put on the gramophone and two of the Edinburgh girls, in the kilt, kicked off their shoes and danced for Granny in their stockings on the slippery linoleum.

4

·

Bochel

·

Every summer when I was a child at the Bochel it came to the time of the peat-cutting. Our moss was out past the Belno farm. Each farm was allocated a moss by the factor and everyone knew their own. Peats were hard at the Bochel moss, much better than the Larryvarry one where they were very brown and soggy. The ashes made by Larryvarry peats were pink instead of grey. One time a car stopped at Woodend and the driver asked Mrs Farquharson what breed her hens were, as they had pink feathers. She had to laugh: 'It's just them cleaning their feathers on the ash midden – they're White Leghorns!' Once a hen which had wandered into the road near Woodend was killed by a car. The driver came in to apologise to Mrs Farquharson. He gave her money so she offered him the hen, but he refused it so she had the money and also the hen for dinner.

Once I had the job of taking soup to the peat moss for dinner. I carried it in a pail with a lid and it was piping hot when I left the Bochel. To save them lighting a fire I ran all the way. It was a very hot day, so while the others ate their soup I lay down to have a rest and fell asleep. I wasn't wearing a hat for the sun, and no one thought to cover my head. On the way home with the others that night I felt sick and my head ached.

I couldn't stand the light in my eyes, so a black curtain was put across the window in the bedroom. Then Granny arrived with the cure – a spoonful of castor oil and an aspirin. I slept all night and was perfectly all right in the morning, but the family spoke about it long after – the day Isobel got sunstroke in the Braes!

Peat-cutting was hard work. Dad worked like lightning with a special spade, throwing the peats out soaking wet and heavy. The rest of us put them on the barrow and wheeled them out twelve at a time. Then we tipped them out in layers. When they were dry on one side we turned them on the other to dry. The next stage gave you backache, setting the peats upright two by two with a clod on top to keep the rain off. A clod was half a peat that had broken. When they dried in good weather we put them into bigger stacks, but in a wet summer they had to be turned inside out – and it usually rains in July.

There was another peat moss at Ladderfoot and also one below the Scalan, over by the hill. Sandy Matheson used to cut and cart the peats and Nellie wheeled them out. It was a great sight at the end of the summer, all the carts going down the road to the different farms and then the building of the stack to last all winter. The last one to work the Belno moss in the old way was Reid the Mill, and his son is still burning peats which are stacked up in the Mill sheds. Nowadays Edward Stuart uses modern machinery at Ladderfoot, and he also runs a peat-cutting business at the Feithmusach between Knockandhu and Tomintoul.

The Society of the Holy Childhood had a picture of a little child climbing the stairs collecting for the missions in Africa. The schoolmaster collected our pennies, and when they came to half a crown the child moved up a step. When we reached the top step the money was sent to a Father Gray in Edinburgh, along with letters he had asked us to send. Over the years there were so many letters from the Bochel that when he visited Chapeltown he asked where it was. Our farm was pointed out to him from the car as he was leaving. He wrote a letter mentioning 'the Bochel, which alas I only saw from afar', and sent us a wooden plaque.

After she finished school, my sister Mary went to work at the Exciseman's house of the Minmore Distillery. She was fourteen when she started and was paid five shillings a week. She walked to Mass at Tombae and came on to have dinner with us at the Bochel. Later, when she was in service at Tomnavoulin, Mary bought a second hand bicycle, and it lasted her seven years. A new bike cost seven pounds in the 1930s.

Jean was twelve years younger than me, and when I left the Braes I used to send her dresses for birthday and Christmas parties. When I went back on holiday she wanted to show me the dresses she had. She went into the bedroom and came through with them all on, one on top of the other. She was very thin then. She would parade round the floor, taking one off to show the next and so on. We all had a good laugh. When Meggie and I sent her party shoes she wrote and said, 'I just danced and danced in them. I was so happy.'

Jean used to sleep-walk when she was worried about her exams. Once she walked down the stairs at the Bochel and was about to go outside. Mam slept in a room on the ground floor by the porch and heard the latch click. She got up, walked Jean upstairs and got her back to bed – didn't wake her.

Jean was a teacher for forty years and then she became a hostess at Glendronach Distillery, Forgue. She looks after the souvenir shop and also does the books. Jean was always a very clever girl. After Chapeltown School she spent three years cycling to the secondary department in Tomintoul before going on to the Sacred Heart at Queen's Cross Aberdeen. Then she went for teacher training to the other Sacred Heart Convent at Craiglockhart in Edinburgh. She knew Cardinal Winning as a young man before he left for Rome to become a priest, because his sister was at Craiglockhart. When they got a weekend off she sometimes took Jean home to the Winning house in Glasgow because it was too far to Glenlivet. I met Cardinal Winning when he came down to say Mass in Westminster Cathedral, and there was a buffet afterwards in St Andrew's Hall. I told him I came from the Braes, and he asked if I knew Jean Bochel. I answered, 'Yes, she's my sister!' He told me he had visited the area himself, staying with the parents of John Copland who was a student with him. Monsignor Copland is now the Vicar General of the Aberdeen diocese.

Our home at the Bochel was sold a few years ago to a lady from London. I was back staying at the Kirkie one year and went up the old farm track for a visit. The lady told me that once it had drifted snow in the night right over the window. When she woke up it was so dark she didn't know if it was night or day. There was still no water indoors or electricity at that time, but for a while the garden was beautifully kept up by Willie McIver with painted double fencing to keep out the cows and sheep. There have been other people at the Bochel since, and it was sold again quite recently. It's a lonely place nowadays, especially in winter, and you can't get a car up in wet weather (never mind in snow) because of the tractor ruts. Of course we never found it lonely when I was young. Mam once said she never heard the grandmother clock tick until all the children were grown up. Charlie took over the farm after Dad retired. Ian Rhindhu has it now (Ian Matheson, that is) and the two farms are run together.

Mam and Dad moved out of the Bochel and went to Millbank when he retired, down to the house beside the Mill, and Granny Bochel died there. At her funeral the coffin was carried from Millbank to the Church – no hearse, just groups of four men taking turns. As the papers reported at the time, Granny Bochel was taken round by the Chapel-house where she had lived when she first came to the Braes. Mam hated being alone at Millbank after Dad died. Louie Milne always came down from Rosemount to stay the night, except when the six Turner girls came up from Edinburgh for the holidays. They were my sister Margaret's daughters. She married Sandy Turner, and he was working down there when Meggie died on 28th March, 1957, two days after the youngest one Ann's second birthday. It was such a sad time, not just for the family but for everyone. When Robbie Lamb reported her death in the *Journal*, he also described the spring that she never saw.

> Deep regret is felt throughout the whole of Glenlivet at the death of Mrs Alexander Turner, at St Raphael's Hospital, Edinburgh, on 30th March, 1957 at the early age of 43. A native of the Braes of Glenlivet, she was a daughter of Mrs Grant of Millbank, Chapeltown. 'Meggie', the name by which she was affectionately known throughout the glen, was bright and friendly – with a zest for life. Her husband, also a native of Glenlivet, is a police officer in Edinburgh. She leaves a family of six, of whom some are of tender years.
>
> As far as it has gone this April is the April that we read about in books but seldom witness. Much of the oat crop has been sown under excellent conditions and the young lambs gambol in the pleasant sunshine. All plant growth is about a month earlier than usual, and the wild birds are busily engaged in nest-making – already several lapwings' eggs have been seen.

Of course the six Turner girls who had lost their mother (my nieces) were given a special welcome whenever they came back north in the school holidays. They wrote to the *People's Journal* about their grandmother, mentioning the boarded-out children she had looked after who came back in summer as adults.

Champion Granny

During the summer months Millbank is never empty. We six sisters spend our holidays in her small cottage. We try to give Gran a holiday – but without success! She is up first in the morning and creeps through to the kitchen to light the fire with sticks and peats. When this has been done she puts on two kettles and soon brings each of us a cup of tea in bed – not forgetting, of course, Dad! From early morning to late evening there is a steady flow of visitors to and from Millbank. The kettle is never off the fire! Each visitor receives a cup of tea – Gran insists on that. In one day we have counted 30 visitors!

Millbank is always full of children. Those children Gran once brought up now have children of their own who visit her. A family of six children live on the other side of the burn during the summer months. We often go for picnics with them. Gran makes sure we have plenty lemonade and food with us. And how she makes us wrap up in case the mist comes down! Beside looking after the six of us Gran looks after her husband, known to everyone as Dad. In the evening, under the light of a lamp – there is no electricity in Millbank – she reads to him. She used to read to Granny Bochel after she reached the age of 100. Should any of us be out late, we never fail to return to find the table set for us and the kettle on the fire. She always leaves a light burning to guide us to Millbank. Gran has, in her own words, 'very kind neighbours'. One lady nearby brings Gran her messages and helps her in the house. Often in winter a young farmer comes to Gran's rescue when she is unable to open the door because of deep snow!

Gran writes quite a number of letters each week (we receive at least one a week in Edinburgh) and she looks forward to the postie coming at 1 p.m. every day. We have often asked if she would like to live with us one day, but we know that the place where she is most happy is 'The Braes o' Glenlivet'. Gran is nearly 80 years of age but she has again invited us to Millbank for two months in summer. She will always try to be up first and bring us tea in bed. She will always be the kind Mam whom so many know and love and to whom they owe so much.

I'll finish with another newspaper cutting because it's hard to write about my mother's last days.

The oldest resident in the Braes of Glenlivet Mrs Elsie Grant, Millbank, celebrates her 90th birthday tomorrow, 28th September, 1975, and tonight a party will be held for all her friends and relations in the Braes Hall. Mrs Grant, who has spent all her life (except for three years in Glasgow) in the Braes, has 14 grandchildren and four great-grandchildren.

At that time Mam went down every winter to stay with my sister Mary's family in Darlington, and it was there that she died on 19th May, 1976. The funeral was at Chapeltown of course. It said in the paper, 'Mrs Elsie Grant (Mam the Bochel) is at rest.'

5
·
Schooldays
·

There were over a hundred pupils at the Braes school in my mother's day, and a notice in each room said 'Accommodation for Sixty Children'. It was opened in 1860. Above the bell is written RELIGIONI AC BONIS ARTIBUS 1860 AD – I think it means we were to learn religion and good skills. There is a stone cross at the gable end. The school closed exactly a hundred years later in 1960 when there were only five children at it. Every house had a large family in the old days: sixteen children in Sandy Matheson's house at the Scalan, sixteen at Belno, and sixteen at Cairnmore – that was the Shop-house. (We thought there were only fifteen there but in the family tree we found a baby called Elspeth who died at a few months old.) The children at school were very healthy. I never knew of a death at our school all the nine years I was there.

Right through school my teachers were a married couple called Mr and Mrs Hornby. She had been Charlotte Mann before she married, and she took the younger children. Mr Edward Hornby was the headmaster and taught the older ones. They were employed by the Priest for several years after they first came to the Braes. The wages were very little – I think it was ninety pounds a year between them. They had to pay rent out of that and employ a girl to cook and clean the house.

Later the Education Authority took over the Catholic schools all over Scotland on condition that the first half hour in school was kept for Religious Education. The Hornbys got much better wages after the change but we lost all our days off for Saints' Days like Saints Peter and Paul, St Andrew and St Joseph. We loved the Catholic feast days as we got the day off school, but that finished when the schools were taken over by the Education Authority. We didn't even get the Glenlivet holiday or the Tomintoul one – only the tattie holiday. It was always arranged for warmer parts of Banffshire, but our potatoes were never ready. However we managed to lift them on a Saturday later on.

What a Catholic education we had! Everyone was prepared for First Confession, First Communion and Confirmation, of course, and Mr Hornby also taught the altar boys Latin. Weekday Mass was at 8.30 in the morning and school didn't start till 9.30, so if children came early they went to Mass. The headmaster locked the School doors, so we were glad to come in to Church if it was a cold day instead of freezing in the playground. The toilets there were called 'the offices'. They were dry, of course, and screened off by corrugated iron for girls and boys. The whole school used to attend all funerals until one day an inspector from Keith turned up at 9.30 a.m. when we were all in Church and the school door was locked. The master was worried when he saw the luxurious car at the school door. After that it changed, but we still got out to funerals if it was a relative.

The Priest would call in at the school at any time of day to ask Catechism questions and make sure we knew our Religious Instruction. On Sundays the school children had to march up to the altar rails after the Gospel. The oldest one handed over the pages we were studying. Of course every child knew then which question they would be asked along the line. If he had asked out of line, there might have been confusion. This was done to let parents know how well we were being instructed. The altar boys stood on the other side of the rail. Their white gowns were always washed and starched by the Stuarts at Crombie Cottage.

On Shrove Tuesday, before Lent began, we got a half-day – home at 2 p.m. – and all the housewives along the roadside made oatmeal brose and pancakes for the children. We tapped on the doors and called, 'Brose and bannocks!' Our mother made oatmeal brose in a big basin and put a thimble, a button and trinkets in the mixture. All the children were given spoons to sup it with, and we hoped to get a silver sixpence if we were lucky, or at least a silver threepenny piece. She covered them all in paper in case we swallowed them.

During Advent we said 4,000 Hail Marys in memory of the 4,000 years people waited for the coming of the Lord. At the same time we wished for something for Christmas. I asked for a doll, and I got it from my aunt in London who didn't know I was praying for a doll. My sister Meggie prayed we would never be without food. Mam took her to the larder on Christmas Eve and there we had rabbits, hare and a couple of grouse. Neighbours were kind, and we had a lot of relatives round the Braes.

Schoolchildren formed the choir at Sunday Mass in the gallery at the back. Mr Hornby had a good bass voice and he loved his choir. Sometimes we were so cold we could hardly sing – my feet were like ice – and it must have been painful to listen to. Two girls, Mary Stuart Easterton and Jeannie McKay, had good voices so they sang solo at Christmas and Easter. At Easter Jeannie sang the Latin hymn 'Regina Caeli'. I loved 'Adeste Fideles' at Christmas, and 'By the First Bright Easter Day' at Easter. Inside the school we had a May Altar with a statue of Our Lady the same as the one above the church door. Children brought flowers for the whole month, and we sang hymns every day – 'Hail Queen of Heaven, the Ocean Star' and 'Bring Flowers of the Rarest'.

We had October Devotions in Church, 7 p.m. for grown-ups and after school at 4 o'clock for us. Some children forgot to bring a head-dress and the teachers would make a fuss about it, so they ran to my mother at Comelybank and she managed a beret or tammy, or else a scarf. Ladies and girls always wore a hat or veil in church then.

nnets for all the little girls at
er with two sections of honey.

art Belno invited three of us to
k. While we were playing she
ies want honey.' Of course we
ne with a whole section cut in
nd. We were very sick after
have taken the honey home
hat a job we had washing our

te for school she heard the
she was still only at the Mill bridge, so she went
granny for flowers. Mr Hornby was all smiles when she
arrived, thinking she had made herself late fetching them. We
only had jam jars for vases. Mary McPherson (who became
Mother McPherson of the Sacred Heart) was late for school
one day. When she was asked why she said 'I was listening to
the larkies singing.' There were always lapwings then but so
few now – perhaps the fertilisers in the fields have killed them
off.

In my mother's day the children all took a peat to school.
There was a bunker in each room but no coal was provided
until after the Education Authority took over the school. I had
to have both coal fires burning brightly by 9.30 a.m. because
Mam was the school cleaner. The cleaners in the Braes got
£3.50 every three months to sweep, dust and wash the porch
with its stone flags. They were supposed to scrub the wooden
floors every six weeks on their hands and knees, but Mr
Hornby wouldn't hear of it in winter – the floors took so long
to dry out and he was afraid it would give him rheumatism. He
would stand right in front of the fire guard. His trousers were
singed with the heat, but we didn't tell him. Our three rows of
desks were a long way back and I could hardly hold the pen,
my hands were so cold. Even when there was snow on the
ground he never asked us to bring the desks nearer. Talking of
desks, the master made me share one with George Stuart

Easterton because we both had fair white hair. I hated it, and later went in with Mary Curran.

I used to pick up little sticks along the avenue among the trees in front of the Church when I couldn't get the fires to burn because the sticks in school were damp. Mrs Lamb's husband chopped sticks for school fires for £2 a year, and then when he retired from that our mother had to provide them. We always had sticks drying round the fire every evening, a special bag for them, and an old rag soaked in paraffin was used to make a blaze. The school coal was hard to light, especially if there were no small bits, and we never wasted the cinders. Mr Hornby showed me how to make a bridge with cinders – newspaper in the middle, then sticks criss-crossed, coal on top, and perhaps a few prayers to make the fire burn in time for 9.30 when school began. If the fires were burning early I went to 8.30 Mass and dusted the fireplaces at nine o'clock.

School Bell Rings for the Last Time in the Braes

They do not do things by half measures in Chapeltown! At the week-end they suffered a sad loss (writes Helen Fisher). Their sturdy little school, where once a hundred pupils at a time filled its classrooms, closed down forever. And what happened? Did they all sit down and cry? They threw a party. Everybody in the village was there plus many others, making the total who sat down to lunch over two hundred. They invited all former pupils and former teachers and several VIPs. As the Director of Education told them, 'You could have allowed the school to go out like a candle guttering to its end. Instead you have done something incorporating an enormous firework. You have gone out in a blaze of glory.'

When our meal was over a historic sound rang out. It was the ringing of the school bell – the clanging muffin-man kind. The teacher who rang it, Miss Mairi Gordon, was bringing us to order for the speeches. As we stopped our chatter and she laid the bell down at her feet, I wondered how many realised that it was the last time that bell would sound its disciplinary note. But there were happier things to listen to, including a remarkable speech by the oldest former pupil Mr John Rattray, aged 88. He stood up, erect as a guardsman, looked round the room with a keen clear eye, and let the reminiscences pour from him. Back down the years he took us, in this very setting, some of the things still there.

'Over in that corner, look,' he pointed, 'is the peat box where every pupil deposited a peat every day in winter to keep the classroom warm. Sometimes we played on the road and a peat would get broken. There was a croft up there, and (with a look at the clergymen sitting near him) I would not say we stole a peat – we took the loan of one occasionally.' Sometimes, greatly daring, they might take one from the teacher's stack, but 'that was dangerous. You didn't do that very often because there would be a heavy penalty if you were found out'. In his day it was the age of big families. Eight or nine children to a family was the usual and there were two families each with fifteen – although as he pointed out, 'They weren't all at school at the same time!' One of the highlights of the year would be the day before the examinations. 'That was the great day for cleaning the school. All the big boys had to carry water from the Crombie (the burn, which is quite a distance from the school) and with stiff brushes the school would be scrubbed out.'

Mrs Hornby did her training at Notre Dame College in Glasgow. She was a very good teacher. Her husband taught in Dundee and they waited to get married until they could get a house with the job. They were in the Braes twenty-three years, and his brother took over the Shop when Charlie Stuart left. Mr Hornby came from a musical family in Buckie and played the organ. He had a good voice, but Mrs Hornby couldn't sing at all. I was called 'Baby' all my schooldays because Mr and Mrs Hornby remembered the day I was born, so all the schoolchildren called me that too. I hated it. The Hornbys stayed in our house at Comelybank for two months while the Schoolhouse was being painted and got ready, and they were always great friends with my mother. One day Mrs Hornby told her I never cried even when I got a slap, so I had to keep it up – just grit my teeth. Mrs Hornby only used a pointer stick on the palm of the hand but Mr Hornby used the strap and sometimes the cane if he thought it was a serious crime.

I well remember the day the girl in charge of putting out the Waverley pen nibs gave me a broken one. Mr Hornby was saying good-bye to the Priest at the door when I turned round to tell the girl I had a broken nib, and as I had a loud whisper he heard me. When he looked round the door I knew I was for it – it was a great offence to talk while the Priest visited. When he came back in I protested strongly that I couldn't write my essay without a pen, but he took down the cane and I got a whack, along with Mary Curran, the girl I spoke to. She wept, but of course I couldn't. My sister Mary got me out of the seat while his back was turned and put my hand under the tap, which took the sting out, but I was worried sick he would turn round and see her helping me. I felt like telling Father Shaw about it. It's a wonder it didn't put us off religion for good.

Mr Hornby knew I was furious. After a few days he came and sat down in the seat beside me but I didn't let on I saw him. I wasn't often slapped but I grieved for all the ones who were. When I was the only girl in the top class Mr Hornby used to ask me to get the strap from the cupboard. He went on teaching and often I slipped it in the desk hoping he would forget. It worked sometimes and a very grateful look on the child's face and a smile was the result. When I was twelve years old Mr Hornby said 'This is your birthday' and gave me half a crown. I daren't tell any of the other children as no one had ever got a penny from him.

Mrs Hornby was kind, though. She used to buy half a stone of every kind of nuts for Hallowe'en. We all called at the Schoolhouse door with a turnip lantern made like a face and a candle inside. We wore false faces and she tried to find out who we were. She looked at our eyes and knew every child. We always wore boys' trousers at Hallowe'en with plenty pockets to hold the nuts. We took extra turnips to knock on the door, but we were asked to bang them on the back door as it would spoil the paint on the front one. Children used to take turnips from the fields for Hallowe'en. It was my grand-uncle Charlie Stuart's they took most from as his croft was nearest the school. After the school bus started bringing children from Knockandhu, one boy used to take a swede every day after school – he was taking it home for his family's hens. He used to hold it up and wave it. I met the boy after he had left school and he said, 'Does that man still hae as good neeps as he used to?' When I told Charlie he just laughed. Charlie had a habit of saying 'Go to Jericho!' During the war the same boy was with the army in Jericho and he sent Charlie a postcard saying, 'I have landed up in the place you were always sending me to.'

In my mother's day all the children got to eat during the day was a quarter of oatcakes in their school-bags for dinner time with a drink out of the school pump to wash it down. The oatcakes must have been pretty well broken to pieces by the time they got to school. Even in our day there were no school dinners, just a slice of bread and jam and a drink of cold water from the playground pump. In later years the teachers put big iron kettles on the fire and the children brought cocoa and milk and sugar so as to have a hot drink to wash down their piece and jam. Children either had butter or jam in these days, as it was considered extravagance to have both. It amazes me when I see people today putting butter on a roll with soup: I always take mine dry. Potato soup was always made with a little margarine on Fridays as no meat was allowed. We could put onion in it, though, and parsley with some vegetables. We even got a cookery class going towards the end of my time at school. Mrs Hornby asked us to bring an egg each to make pancakes. One girl, Meg Westerton, when she was at Broombank, put too much baking soda in the pancakes she made but we ate them up anyway. There were so many eggs that we took some to the Shop and bought sweets to share.

Every child left school at fourteen, some of them very clever but there was no chance then of getting further education – such a waste of brains. Fathers wanted their oldest son to carry on the farms and crofts, because if they left they would never return. In time, some of the girls went on to be trained as teachers, including my sister Jean, but most boys worked on farms around home. Mr Hornby once asked us to write an essay about what we would like to be when we left school. We knew that there was no further education for girls at the time but all of us wrote the same, that we would like to be a nanny. Christine from the Easterton, known as Bunty, wrote, 'If they are naughty I will smack them', and he put at the bottom, 'Nannies are not allowed to smack.'

I was bored by the time I left school because I was the only one left in the top class and got no lessons. I spent my time cleaning out drawers and the schoolmaster's desk. I had started school at four years old so it was a waste of time staying till the following summer for my fourteenth birthday. I tried to persuade a girl called Lena to stay on with me, but she was a little older and she got an exemption to help her mother at Belno. She lives at Aberlour now. Lena used to make me sit at the roadside and work out sums for her on Tuesdays after school. There was homework every night. I remember it was arithmetic on Tuesday, a map to draw on Thursday and always an essay at the weekend. I did mine on Friday evening so as to be free for the weekend. We always had plenty to do on the farm after school. Sometimes I left my school bag behind the sofa at Crombie Cottage because it was too heavy to carry home to the Bochel. I was so glad to get an exemption at thirteen myself, after being ill, and I never went back.

So that was a disappointing way to end my schooldays, but they were mostly good. Teachers were such strict disciplinarians in those days. We always knew when the schoolmaster arrived in a temper as his hat was on at a sharp angle. They were excellent teachers, though, and I'm glad we all had a good education at Chapeltown School. One boy who joined the Scots Guards when he grew up, Charlie Grant, was very grateful for the education he got at Chapeltown. The soldiers were given a map of the world to fill up – town names and so on. The English ones had no idea where any place was. It all stood us in good stead. No one from our school ever came up before the courts, and the local bobby had so little work to do that his garden was the best for miles around.

6

·

Customs

·

We always had porridge for breakfast. When the cows went dry in the winter because they were expecting calves, we got seeds from the Distillery and made ale the colour of Coke to put on our porridge. There were bottles all over the mantelpiece, and sometimes when this ale fermented the cork popped out and the froth went over the ceiling. Children were sometimes allowed to put a little melted butter or margarine over their porridge instead of milk. We also got sowens from the Distillery – very sweet to taste. We used to love the pease-meal brose. You only needed very little in the bottom of a bowl, and when the boiling water went on it swelled to the top of the bowl. It was tasty with milk.

When girls married, their mothers provided the bed linen, blankets and pillows. The blankets were woven from the fleeces of their own sheep. Feathers for pillows came from the hens when they were killed. People dried the feathers in the oven range if they had one. Pillow-cases were made from flour bags, which were very strong. The brand was Cock of the North, and the pink cockerel on the bag faded after a few washings. They would be laid out for bleaching on the heather, and when the sun was shining we took a watering can and sprinkled them. The pillow-cases ended up lily white.

In the old days people couldn't afford a hotel reception, so the wedding feast was held at the home of the bride's parents. The last one I remember was the McGillivrays' at Achnascraw. Soup was followed by chicken, potatoes and vegetables, finishing up with dessert and cream. Wedding dances were held in the barn of the bride's house, also the reception. Telegrams were read out by the Priest, but only the respectable ones – the best man looked through them first. Granny Bochel liked a telegram which read 'May your love be as deep as the snow on the ben, and your troubles as few as the teeth of a hen.' At her wedding my sister Meggie had 'May you have more than a fence running round your garden' (she was mother to the six Turner girls) and 'May the deer season never end or the grouse season start'.

There were no honeymoons – the new husband was back at his work next morning and the bride began her life as a housewife. Boys played tricks on the newlyweds and blocked the chimney so when the bride lit her first fire in the morning smoke billowed out and had to be cleared before breakfast. That happened to Willie Belno and Bell. Luckily there was always a ladder in the shed, and the bridegroom would be up on the roof clearing the chimney. There was no other means of cooking but on the fire. Farming folk never had holidays, although the men were given a day off for the sales of sheep and cattle at Tomintoul. People had no one to take over looking after the animals. They were quite happy staying at home with their families. In our day you could live on a croft for half a crown a week, because you could grow your own potatoes, vegetables and corn and keep hens and cows for milk.

No one thought of getting married until they had a house to go to and money saved. I remember a priest saying from the pulpit once that even a bird builds a nest before starting a family. The man was the breadwinner – women never went out to work. A man would have been ashamed if he couldn't provide for his wife and family, whatever the size. The larger the family, the prouder the father became and boasted how clever his children were. There were no old people's homes then. Granny sat at one side of the fire and granddad at the other. They were very handy as baby-sitters but parents said they 'ruined' the children.

When Nan at Woodend was newly married she had a visit from John Ledingham and thought she would use her silver teapot. Every bride got one in those days – of course it was only silver-plated. She put it down to warm on the brick in front of the fire while she laid the tea things on the table. She went to infuse the tea and poured the water on top of the tea leaves. When she picked up the teapot, water poured out – it had started to melt! She ran to the scullery with it, hoping John didn't notice, and brought back a china one. Every time he saw her after that he teased her about the incident. Nan also bought one of the small bags of white sugar we got in those days. She put it up in the loft above the living room, but didn't realise it was above the fireplace end till she saw drips on the ceiling. The sugar had started to melt, just like the teapot.

The wives baked every week. Every farm had a kist or bunker with a division in the middle – flour on one side, oatmeal on the other – to last the winter for making oatcakes and scones. Clootie dumplings were made for birthdays instead of birthday cakes. Once when Mam mentioned it was Our Lady's birthday, John Emmett, a boy who was boarded out with her, said, 'Are we getting a dumpling?' Every house had a cheese press outside. The kebbocks were a standby for the winter, and when butter was plentiful it was salted and kept in stone jars to last all winter. The butter pats had the name of the farm on it when they were sold at the Shop, or if not all sold, Walker's bought it to make their cakes.

Farms and crofts had a fan for taking off the ears from corn. The chaff wasn't wasted as we stuffed it fresh into mattresses every year because they got dusty after a while. The tick mattress had to be very full, as it flattened out later. The same went for pillows, which were stuffed with the small soft feathers from hens. At a threshing, two horses did the turning of the wheel while the farmer fed the mill with sheaves. One man handed the sheaves over to him and another watched the corn coming through, lifted the corn box and emptied it into a sack. There was a fourth man forking the straw and taking it off, also someone to tramp the straw down, and of course someone had to drive the horses. The threshing took six people, and they had to work fast. Later on it was done by steam power.

The Steam Mull

Two men hurry along the road to the farm where the threshing is to take place. As they go they see others making in the same direction, for it is the custom for all neighbours to turn out to help with 'the steam mull'. The high speed mill, with its two operatives, requires a good staff to keep it going.

'Ye're a bittie slack the day, boys,' says Jock, the senior of the mill men, with a twinkle in his eye, 'but if ye work weel noo we'll seen get on wi't. Ye can start ony time, Bob.'

'Right ye are, sir,' says Bob, and sets his tractor engine in motion. Although the combination threshing plant is still spoken of as a 'steam mull', the tractor has replaced the steam engine as power generator.

Forkers are soon in position to pitch sheaves from the stacks on to the feeding bench. 'Lowsers' get ready to cut the twine bands and hand the sheaves to the feeder. The 'corn man' sets his sacks in place, and the squad who are to take charge of the straw plan the foundation of their 'soo'. Soon the whirr of the high speed drum mingles with the chuk chuk of the tractor, and all hands are busy.

'Fat like's the corn, Geordie? Good. Man, what a stoor, an' rare halesome stuff. I never thought it wid thresh as weel's that up here in Glenlivet. Tattie corn, is it?'

'Aye, aye, the tattie corn dis best wi' us up here.'

'That's a weel biggit stack, Charlie.'

'Michty aye, min, sheaves near stannin' straught up, rare hearted. Mac can fairly pit them up.'

'Foo's the laads at the strae daen?'

'Richt enough. Corrie's pittin up a fine soo.'

'Hello, Jeck, jist hame for a whilie's leave, are ye?'

'Jist that, Jamie.'

'Dinna work ower hard then.'

'Nae fear o' that. But I like fine to get a turn back amo' the corn and strae.'

'Stoppin' time, boys, we're gaun to get a bite o' denner. Haud awa' doon tae the hoose. Onything fresh wi' the news the day Willie? Oor wireless battery's clean deen.'

'Aye is there, man, the Roosians hes trappit ten German diveesions in the middle Neeper.'

'Man, that's graun. That Roosians can fairly fecht. Gude general that Vitootin. I hope he seen caa's Hitler's Huns hame tae the faa'n doon bomb-blasted hole that wis Berlin.'

'Come awa' than, boys, we'll need tae be yokin' again,' cries Jock, the mull boss. 'Ye hae eaten plenty and gabbit plenty, come and work noo.'

The afternoon wears on, the ricks of oats get fewer, and as the February twilight begins to fall the threshing is finished. Groups of workers gather round the mill and tractor to examine them. Pipes are lit; blast, drum and elevators are discussed, along with the amount of corn threshed and the quality of the straw. Soon the assistants prepare to go home.

'Mony thanks, laads,' says the farmer as they move off. Aye, aye, Mac, man, ye're welcome. Dod, Corrie's pat a fine croon on that strae.'

R. L., Glenlivet

Jeems's Mary gave me a gold ring with the letter M on – it would have been better given to either of my sisters, whose initial was M. I wore it to school, which didn't please the schoolmaster, or 'maister' as we called him. He thought it very forward for my age, which was thirteen. However I lost it when I was tramping the straw at the Bochel threshing. It really was like looking for a needle in a haystack. I expect a cow swallowed it.

When I was still quite young and living at Comelybank, I used to help by turning the wheel of the fan when the chaff was taken from the corn. It was called winnowing. One time when Jeems called 'Wo!' I let go the handle but didn't stand far enough back. It caught me in the stomach and I was tipped over into the chaff. I wasn't hurt, as it was nice and soft, but Mary and Jeems got quite a fright.

Everything used to be done locally. Two tailors worked full-time making the men's tweed suits, which were more suitable for the climate than the blue serge suits the young men started to wear on Sundays. In the old days men only shaved on Sundays. The tailors worked in a shed at the back of the wash-house at the Shop. Once a new tailor arrived to lodge in a house somewhere. He met a girl and asked her the way. She directed him, and he made a date with her for the next night. He wasted no time. They later married – that was Johnny Russell's parents. Later on he had the Shop. There were also two shoemakers – Charlie Stuart Comelybank and Charlie Rattray at Springlea. I believe there was also a McHardy shoemaker at the Scalan, but long before my time. Even coffins were made locally, at Eskemore Croft, and when the Shop was finally closed in 1966 Johnnie Russell came across a shroud in the attic.

> Mr John Russell, merchant and sub-postmaster at Chapeltown, Braes of Glenlivet, for more than 17 years, has retired from business. At a small gathering he was presented with a cocktail cabinet, a gift from the community, by Mr William Stuart, Belno. Mrs Russell was presented with chocolates by Mr Charles Grant, Bochel. Mr Russell recalled that he had started in the Shop as a boy at a shilling a day. After serving in World War I he spent 18 years in Montana. Eventually he returned to his native glen and bought the Braes Shop.

Johnnie Russell and his wife Dolly retired to the Schoolhouse. The Shop was great in my Uncle Charlie Stuart's day. Three girls and two men were working there, and it never closed at lunch-time. They took their meals at different times. My sister worked there in Mr Hornby's day and had three lunches – the school-children, then Mr and Mrs Hornby, then Willie Robertson and Dora Hornby. When Mr Hornby was in charge of the Shop before the war he used to sell red Canadian apples which were polished up and put on display. There were oranges too, and once when one was bad he gave it to his little boy Eddie and told him to throw it in the midden. Eddie was full of mischief. He saw Willie the Mill coming down the road past

Roughburn and threw the orange at him. It landed right on his ear, and when Willie arrived at the Shop door to report him he was still picking the bits out. Eddie got a thrashing, of course.

There was none of today's fuss over greetings cards and the Shop didn't sell any, but one thing the housewives liked was wallpaper. A new sample book of patterns came out every year ready for the spring-cleaning. There were all kinds of modern papers, and the borders were so rich with leaves and fruit that they cost more than the wallpapers. Whenever the merchant at the Shop got a new book he gave away the last year's one. In those days all the houses had an outside toilet, and we were the same at the Bochel. My sister Mary papered the toilet at the bottom of the garden with all the different sheets of wallpaper. She just made a paste with flour and water to stick them on. She papered the inside of the door as well because it was draughty. One winter night we had a bad gale and the roof blew off, but Dad just laid an old door on top.

The Shop had a glass case full of lovely things and there were rimmed spectacles in it. When the older men's sight was failing they tried a pair on and read a bit of the newspaper. The glasses just magnified the print and they cost a shilling. When anyone died other men would call at the house and ask for the spectacles, saying, 'I could see well with his'. They never had their eyes tested.

Mr and Mrs Lamb used to come to the Shop together every Friday from Larryvarry to collect their ten shilling pensions. She had a job getting him home, because he liked to stop for a drink. Bass strong beer cost a shilling a bottle then. She drove him up the road in front of her, and now and again he pretended to turn back. I expect he had managed to have one drink, and was only teasing her. She was tiny and he was a tall man, very handsome.

The Shop was a meeting place for the men on a Saturday night – much handier than the Pole. A mason called Henry Smith was working at Rhindhu, and after he got paid he visited the Shop and stayed till he was very drunk. He lived at Woodside Cottage round the back of Tamvoan wood. We children watched him staggering up above Easterton. For every step forward he took two back, and fell many times. It took him about an hour to get up that brae through all the stones. We asked his daughter Maggie how he got home. She said his trousers were all torn and his legs were scratched. He had boilings in his pocket for the children and they were broken to matchwood. It's a wonder he didn't break his legs, but he was well upholstered.

There was a McPherson at the Glack who visited Geordie Stuart Easterton, where they had bees, and he was given a comb of honey to take home with him for the children. He had nine, so he gave each one a spoon and laid the honey-comb on the table. After a while he heard them saying to each other, 'Do you like honey?' They got very sick with it. This same man was visiting us at Comelybank one time. Granny had the latest invention, a stone hot water bottle, and he fancied one for his wife. He carried it home to the Glack all right to show her, but he'd had a few drinks at the Shop and was seeing double so he missed the table and it landed on the cement floor.

A molecatcher used to go around the farms all the time. He lived in Tomintoul, and got the name Moley though his name was Grant – he married Mary McHardy from Tomnareave. Moley died years ago but his son who had the garage in Tomintoul still gets called Young Moley. When boys caught moles they used to skin them and nail them to the barn door to stretch them and then sold them for a shilling each. Moleskin coats were popular then.

The boys also used to make money selling rabbit skins. A man came up from Glasgow to stay at Glackan, the top house at Knockandhu on the right-hand side, and collected them round the farms. The skins were all dried off in the shed. Rabbits were also sent to Purvey's, a game dealer in London's East End. We all collected plovers' eggs in the spring and ate them hard-boiled. We called the birds 'peeweeps' because their song was like that. If the gamekeeper caught you, you were fined fifteen shillings because they were getting scarce. I believe the whites of their eggs were sometimes made into glue, but at Claridge's in London they were a great delicacy at dinner.

When visitors called at the Braes houses they always went to the back door, because the wife was usually in the kitchen and wouldn't hear a knock at the front. When the new priest Father Shaw called for the first time he went to the front door at Easterton. The wee boy of the family Alistair Stuart, who was only four, saw him. No one heard the knock, so he called up at him, 'Go round to the back door, you bugger!' After that, when Alistair was at school, the Priest would point at him in his seat and the poor boy would blush.

7
.
Families

.

The McPhersons at Corrunich are descended from the family of Abbé McPherson, who built the first church at Chapeltown. Elsie was the one who carried me at my christening because Lena, my godmother, was only ten. Peter went to stay at Knockandhu with his wife. They had no family of their own but took boarded-out children. Willie McPherson was offered a farm on Deeside, so Elsie went to be his housekeeper. Then he gave up farming and became a school janitor in Aberdeen. Mary McPherson worked for the Stuarts at Roughburn when Lena, Agnes and Ian were children. One of the McPherson brothers (Charles, I think) went to London and was given the job of shepherd in Richmond Park. A wealthy girl who used to ride there fell in love with him. They married, and bought a farm in Wiltshire run on very modern lines. Then they retired and went to live in Aboyne, and the two daughters were sent to the Sacred Heart boarding-school at Kilgraston near Perth. One went on to be a nun and her photo was in the local paper. The McPhersons were a very good-looking family.

John McPherson went away to be a priest. He was a curate in the Cathedral at Aberdeen before getting his own parish at Aboyne. Then the First World War came along and he became a chaplain with the army. After the war he went to America. Another McPherson brother, Donald, went to the USA with my Uncle Walter and stayed with him all his life. He never married, but Walter did and he and his wife Barbara had a boy and a girl. My sister Mary met Donald over there. They were in Detroit, then North Dakota, and ended up in Oregon. I went to visit Uncle Walter in Oregon, but Donald had died by then.

Sophia McPherson worked at the Chapel-house and was engaged to a man called Luke Grant who went to Canada. When she heard he was coming home she said, 'Long looked for, come at last!' They married and went back there. Charlie, Sophia and Annie McPherson all came back for a holiday just before the war. They stayed with their sister Libbie at Clashnoir – the house is gone now. I met them going for a picnic on a Wednesday, which was half-day at the shop so they had no biscuits. It was a lovely sunny day and I suggested they should go up to The Drovers above the Scalan. They said it was all too sad. Their old family home was now a ruin so they couldn't go there.

Maggie Stuart was a half-sister of my mother's – both from the family of sixteen at the Shop. Maggie was a full sister of Lena's father Charlie Stuart, who had the Shop in the Braes until he took a farm at Peterculter. She went to teach in the Catholic school at Braemar and met her husband there.

My cousins May and Violet McDonald grew up in Braemar. May became a nanny to the Brand family in Edinburgh. Jim Brand was an actor before he became a priest. He was at my parish church for a while (that's Ogle Street in London) and got the people to put on 'Murder in the Cathedral'. It ran for three nights and he was in it. He had women on the stage – normally the altar – but all they had to do was moan and groan. Father Brand was a most amusing man who thought priests should smile and not look gloomy. Once I saw him at a wedding in Kensington and he was beaming with smiles all the time.

May married David Kenny in 1937, and they had a boy then

twin girls, and finally a boy called David. May took them back
to Braemar for safety during the war. Their son David was only
ten when his father died. He became an electrician and
emigrated to Edmonton, Canada, where he married a girl
from the cycling club and they had five children. May went
over to Edmonton twice when he sent her a ticket through the
bank. Violet McDonald became a Sister of Charity in Millhill,
where she took the name in religion of Sister Clare. She taught
in their schools and was Mother Superior of more than one
convent in London. A few weeks before her death at the age of
91 I met her again at May's house in Ruislip, when the three of
us watched the video of my 80th birthday party in the Braes
Hall. Shortly after that May herself died at 94.

Mary Keenan was Pat Keenan's daughter. He and his brother
Andrew were boarded out with the McHardys at Bankhead, a
tiny house opposite Burnside, where there is now a place for
dipping sheep. Mrs McHardy also had two sons of her own.
One of them, James McHardy, moved to Corrunich when he
married Bell, Jessie Beattie's sister, and took the roof off the
other house. They all did that in those days so as not to pay
rates. Mary grew up at the gamekeeper's house on the
Gallowhill, above the Minmore Distillery. Mary's grandmother,
Nellie Grant, lived at a wee house in the heather called Strans,
and Mary's mother, another Nellie Grant, was born there. It
was at Invernahaven opposite Belno, and she came back as
Miss Grant California after living in America. Later, this grandmother (she was a widow, Mrs Morrow) came to live at a house
called Clemmie's, where the Braes Hall is now. She had a dog
called Fido, and the two of them lived there on her ten shilling
pension. After a while she got old and lost her memory, but
neighbours helped until eventually she was taken to Nazareth
House in Aberdeen.

Georgie Stuart was in my class at school. Like myself he hadn't
far to come, from Easterton opposite the Church. East
Auchavaich is the farm's real name, according to the factor's
office, but we all called it Easterton. It was Father Shaw who

suggested that the Stuarts should move to a farm on the Blairs estate outside Aberdeen with their nine children. When they left, one of the sons, Jim Easterton, walked their two plough-horses over the hills all that way. There were no horse boxes then. I'm sure the father was broken-hearted at leaving the Braes. We were certainly very sad when the family left as it was a loss of eleven natives. His wife belonged to Riv, beside Ladderfoot. It was his big brother Alistair we used to watch practising for the Highland Games events before he became a famous athlete. Then there were Jim and Frances who went to Aberdeen. The others I remember are Mary, Jessie, Margaret, Bunty and Douglas. Mam was godmother to Douglas, who was about two when the family left. Christine stayed at the Lettoch during the war with her two children, and Georgie also came back on visits – these two were both about ages with me at school.

Mary and Peter Cumming at Belno of Tomalienan were rel-atives on my father's side, and their sister Annie Cumming was at Culantuim. She knitted black gloves for the Pope every New Year, beautifully done in three-ply wool. My grandfather John Stuart and Alex Stuart the Mill were going to Rome one year so they took the gloves to deliver them. In those days you got a personal audience with the Pope. There weren't the crowds then as people didn't have money to go abroad. I still have the photograph of the audience when they got the papal blessing down to the fourth generation. I thought the three-tiered hat he wore was lovely. Popes don't wear it now.

They were very good Catholics in that family. Sandy Grant was married to a Cumming sister who died, and Annie brought up her baby. We called him young Sandy. His father was my grandfather's brother on my father's side of the family, and they had a sister, Mrs Hay of Keith. Mary and Jessie Hay worked in the woollen mills there and used to come on holiday to Comelybank. I remember when they brought their nephews to visit us at Comelybank. Francis died in the war – he was in the RAF. Old Sandy Grant was a lovely man with a beard. A sister of

Sandy's, Mrs Hay of Keith, used to come on holiday to Culantuim with her two daughters, Mary and Jessie. Eventually they took Annie away to Keith when she was too old to look after herself. Mary and Jessie used to come to us for holidays at Comelybank, and then later they went to Calier.

People have always come back in search of their families. A man called Ian Cameron of Dundee discovered that he had ancestors in the Braes through Flora McDonald Achdregnie, who was a schoolteacher in Dundee. This was in the 1930s. He was a great hiker and he walked across the hills from Dundee to Braemar, where he stayed in the Youth Hostel. The next night Ian was in Tomintoul Hostel, and then he walked to Achdregnie where Mrs McDonald (who was Mary the Mill) sent him up past Glack, Lagual and Badevochal to Westview. He said to Mrs Robertson there, 'I think I'll find all my relatives in the cemetery,' but she sent him on up to the Bochel because our mother had married her brother George Grant. He came to us a lot on holiday after that.

The Mill of Achnascraw

At the Church door after 11 o'clock Mass one Sunday a lady called out, 'Does anyone remember Meg o' the Mill?' She was visiting from Vancouver with her sister and her son, a priest called Father Jim Comey. Jessie Robb (that was Jessie Beattie) stepped forward, and she and her sister Bell took them up for tea to Daisy Cottage on the Carracks. They took photos of Jessie and Bell and went away with Maisie the Mill's address at Lossiemouth.

Young Alex Stuart the Mill went to the Abbey School at Fort Augustus for two years. His mother had a job managing him after the father died, so Father Shaw took him away to the school as a boarder. He wrote home and asked her to send his bicycle. In those days a railway van called at the Shop from Ballindalloch Station. When she looked out of the window a few days later there was Alex. He had cycled all the way from Fort Augustus. Two other millers carried on for some years after the father died, but then there was no more meal mill. Nobody grows corn now, but it was nice to have your own oatmeal.

Another time when Father Comey was over with his mother and aunt, they visited Lucy and Mairi Gordon. Mairi was the last teacher in the Braes. Meg o' the Mill was sister to my grandfather at the Shop. Meg lived in the Cabrach when she first married, and then when her husband died she went to Canada and opened a grocer's shop. Another sister of Meg's (Jean, I think) married a McGillivray, and they lived in the top house in Knockandhu on the right-hand side. She would be Gordon McGillivray Achnascraw's great-grandmother.

The McGillivrays were a large family at Cartach, Knockandhu. I can remember Jean, Maggie, Nellie, Geordie, Charlie and Willie. Charlie was the father of Ian McGillivray – Ian came back from Glasgow to live at Chapeltown in the modern house he built called Craigdhu.

A dance was held in the Braes of Glenlivet Public Hall on the evening of New Year's Day 1959. Tea was handed round by a band of willing helpers, and a large company spent an enjoyable evening dancing to the music of the Gay Timers Band from Tomintoul. Mr C. McGillivray, sen., of Craigdhu was MC.

The McGillivrays moved into the farm of Achnascraw from Tomnareave croft, and Gordon McGillivray still has Achnascraw. John McGillivray moved to the croft at Tomnareave when he married my grand-aunt, Jane Ann Stuart, from Christivoan. They had seven children and Louise went to live in Keith in a house which she called Tomnareave. The old McGillivray place at Tomnareave has gone, but there were four houses there at one time. James Lamb had one, then Nellie Michie, and McGillivray's was joined on to the house of Kirsty Grant who became Mrs Drysdale.

In the old days, if a couple had no children and you had a big family you gave them one to bring up, and that happened to the McGillivray father. He had been fostered to a Protestant family, so none of his children were brought up as Catholics. His family went to Tombae school and knew all the Catholic prayers, although they were Protestant and Tomnavoulin School was nearer. Then Charlie McGillivray went to work at Easterton in the Braes. Being so close to the Church, and living in a Catholic family, Charlie came to all the services – not just Mass on Sundays, but May and October Devotions and Stations of the Cross. He became a convert before he married. The little house at Knockandhu is gone now, and instead there are two army huts turned into a house with sheds all around. James McGillivray was an uncle to this family, and he lived first at Badevochel then Demick.

I knew Nellie McGillivray as Mrs Sutherland when I met up with her in Edinburgh in about 1954 – she had a picture of the Sacred Heart above her bed and often visited the Sacred Heart church at Lauriston. Meg stayed on at Cartach and Geordie moved down to Dufftown. Willie went away to Canada with his wife and children. Jean went first to Minmore but then moved to Aberlour when she married. I met a man at Tombae one time who said he was a scoutmaster from Aberlour on his way to visit boys camping at the beauty spot below Achdregnie. He was bringing them chocolate bars. He told me he was Jean McGillivray's son, and I could see he was very like Ian and Charlie.

There is a wonderful picture of the congregation at the Church opening in 1897. My mother was born in 1886 and would have been about eleven years old, so she must be one of the little girls. The only ones I recognise are my uncle at the Shop and Charles Stuart Demick, the one with the long beard, who retired to Comelybank. He wasn't related to us, although he married Helen Stuart the Mill. Their son was Charlie Stuart who retired to Comelybank and married Mary at Crombie Cottage. Then there was Jim Stuart Eastertown who lives in Aberdeen and has a daughter. His wife died and he went to live with his sister Frances. When he was fit for it Jimmy always used to come and walk round the Braes for a day every year. He's a few years older than me. When the pools were covered in ice on the Carracks he used to take us up to skate on moonlight nights.

8

.

Winter

.

People nowadays can hardly imagine what winter used to be like in the Braes. There were no snow ploughs, just road men digging with spades. Then the wind would blow in the night and fill the road with snow again. But we always had a peat fire in the grate. There was no coal, no one could afford that, but there was plenty wood if you liked to drag it from Tomvoan or the Bochel. When we were at Comelybank we made bundles of branches of beardie green bits that burned great on washing day. Bunty Stuart came with us, and climbed to the top of the tree and broke them down with her feet, then slid down to the ground. She did enough for all our bundles. She didn't worry when she tore the dress her mother had knitted for her.

In the old days people were sensible enough to have plenty of food in the house as winter approached in case they were snowed in. Every household had a bag of flour to make scones and pancakes as well as loads of oatmeal in a kist, so it didn't matter if the baker couldn't get through with loaves. We loved treacle scones, and one time we used the cows' treacle which was meant for their winter feed. It was a serious business if the winter feed ran out.

A helicopter from RNAS Lossiemouth ran a shuttle service to and from the isolated farm of Fuerandearg, Braes of Glenlivet, yesterday carrying fodder to starving livestock. The owner of the farm, Mr Robert Lamb, had trekked two miles to Chapeltown to phone for assistance to the SSPCA, who contacted the naval station. Mr Lamb and his neighbours dug a twenty-five yard long letter A – the emergency code – and lit a bonfire to guide the helicopter down. Back from the hour-long flight to and from the farm, the 'copter pilot Lieut. John Maguire said conditions were pretty bad in the area. 'There are still heavy hail and snow storms,' he said. 'There didn't appear to be a road or path open anywhere near the farm. In fact the nearest clear road must have been about five miles away.' Four drops were made yesterday and two more are expected to take place today. A ton and a half of hay will be dropped altogether.

Jeannie McKay's Uncle Robbie lived at Clashnoir Cottage. In winter he plugged the keyhole with cotton wool when the wind was howling round the house, as there was no porch then. After one bad storm the baker came to a house in Tomintoul where the snow was so deep he couldn't open the door, so he called through the chimney to take her order. At Larryvarry, Mrs Lamb, who started married life in Edinburgh, went out one morning to a huge mound of snow outside the front door. She climbed to the top of it and called out, 'Abraham, Isaac and Jacob come and take me out of here!' but they never came. Her husband was often away working at Inchrory, above Tomintoul. She would say, 'Him in Inchrory and me left with all to do.' She was tiny and he was six feet four.

It hurt the farmers when the Duke of Richmond and Gordon gave up the Glenlivet Estate in lieu of death duties before the last war. The old Duke was kind to the tenants, but unfortunately the family had two deaths in seven years. When word got out that the old Duke had died Annie Cumming said, 'What a pity, and it the only juke about the Shop.' She thought the duck had died, as we called ducks 'jukes'. When Crown Lands became the landlord they doubled the rents. The worst came after the war when the Forestry Commission took over

the woods which had always provided shelter for farm animals in the snow. Each farm round Tomvoan wood – Achnascraw, Rhindhu, Demick, Belno, Corrunich, Auchavaich and Easterton – had their own bit fenced off. One very bad winter the farmers opened the gates and let their cows in.

Winter Survey from the Braes of Glenlivet by Robert Lamb Although the official season of winter 1962 is behind us we are still labouring under semi-Arctic conditions. Only small patches of mother earth are free from snow, with slight fresh falls an almost daily occurrence. The weather clerk extended our winter season at both ends, for the first heavy snowfall came on 2nd December. March has been our worst month. Softly the lion advanced, paws well padded with snow, until the ground was buried to a depth of 15 inches. By the 8th Leo was roaring, with a south-west hurricane which hurled the snow into deep hard-packed drifts. These blocked all roads and brought traffic to a standstill. Side roads are still impassable.

A fairly good supply of fodder made the handling of stock not too much of a problem but sheep have had some severe conditions, especially during March when the deep snow kept them from foraging on the ground. This is always serious to Blackfaced sheep, and there are a few cases of pre-lambing disorders. Weather conditions did not permit a great deal of turnip-lifting to be done and the excessive frosts have damaged a good many, but ewes are mostly in fairly good fettle. Given generous weather the lambing could be an average one.

Wildlife has fared not badly. A few brown hares have died but they are still numerous, so possibly nature has been weeding the weaklings out. Deer have not been much in evidence, and white hares are scarcer than in recent years. Grouse, wild pigeons and the crow family seem to have been little affected, while sparrows and kindred souls have eked out an existence round the stackyards. Our Spring visitors have received a cold welcome. Oyster catchers huddle in small packs by the burn sides, lapwings fly around and pitch on any green spots, and the legs of the curlew look extremely long as he stands on a snow bank and surveys his territory.

Once when there was a lot of snow we made a lovely slide on a brae by the schoolmaster's peat stack. It was a beauty, really wide, but Mr Hornby went out in the dark with the hen's pot and fell on it, rolling down the slide. He didn't really hurt himself, but next morning he put half a stone of salt on and melted the slide. The same happened another time when we made one on the road. It wasn't dangerous, but someone salted and sanded it. When there was likely to be drifting snow Mr Hornby let us out at two o'clock, and of course we were delighted with that. When wellingtons were first worn to school we had to take them off and put on slippers – it would have been bad to wear sweaty rubber all day.

We normally didn't get out till four, except the children from Glen Suie. They were allowed out half an hour early in winter so as to get home before dark. Their father was a gamekeeper. When there was snow he tied them together in the morning so the youngest wouldn't get lost. It was three miles down from the hills. The Innes family lived up there, also Helen Roy and the Hendersons. Evelyn Innes was a gamekeeper's daughter in the Suie. She belonged to a large family, and when both parents died the children were all separated. Evelyn didn't get on with the aunt she was with, so she boldly asked for an exemption from school at thirteen and got a job in service. A shepherd called McPherson lived in a cottage in the Suie, and Mary McPherson and her sisters Sophia and Ella went to stay up there with him in summer. That family were all girls. In fact there was only one boy among all the girls in the Suie. He was called 'The King of the Glen' – he grew into a big lad and became a blacksmith at Burgie near Elgin.

We loved getting a ride on a sledge, especially a horse-drawn one. Two boys called Johnnie Farquharson and his cousin Willie Grant had a big dog called Oscar which pulled their sledge. They invited us to take a ride, but when we came to a big wreath of snow at Roughburn they gave each other a wink and tipped us out into the snow. The two of them made off laughing with Oscar and the sledge, while we shook off the snow. We were not amused. The same two boys made a large snowball at the top of the field above Woodend one winter and rolled it all the way down. It grew bigger and bigger until it was huge, so they told us, and it ran into the back of the house with such a crash that dishes fell off the dresser and smashed. Of course the boys got one of their regular hidings.

Winter was a time for get-togethers and concerts, until television killed them off just when the Braes Dramatic Society was at its peak. They were given great write-ups in the papers.

> Up at Chapeltown the amateur dramatic society are busy preparing their 1953 winter production, this year an ambitious play 'Johnny Jouk the Gibbet' by James Scotland. With the sturdy independent approach they bring to everything up there, they make no pretensions at modesty about such a choice. 'We want all drama societies for miles around to know

that we are doing it,' says their producer Father George Phillips with the air of a challenger. This is The Braes Players' seventh season, and with the healthy rivalry of such small communities they are boasting of the fact that 'Tomintoul has no play this year, nor Glenlivet.' The scene of their preparations for Johnny Jouk is described in these words: 'Keen enthusiasm, good fun and laughter round the blazing peat fire at rehearsals as the storm rages without!'

9

·

Incomers

·

Allsorts of people came in to the Braes of Glenlivet over the years. The earliest ones I can remember were tramps. Packy Sim was a tramp who used to arrive every year. If the people in houses on the roadside saw him coming they locked the door, because once he came in he would sit for hours. Packy occupied every chair – one for his cap, another for his coat, one for his scarf and another to sit on. He would open his pack, and of course you had to buy something. He got his tea and a piece of loaf and jam, but I suppose he was also tired and needed a rest.

Geordie Taylor was another tramp, a nice old man – good-looking with a long beard. He would have a drink at the Pole on his way in to the Braes, and he used to sing 'The Cabin with the Roses at the Door'. He told us he left home at seventeen and had walked all over Scotland – he loved the countryside.

When he was really old he stopped coming. I expect he went to an old folks' home somewhere. There were no government handouts in the old days. Tramps just lived on what people gave them in the way of food and clothes.

Tinkers were different, and travelled in families. There were two farms in the Braes where the tinks were always made welcome, the Bochel and Auchavaich, when the Grants were there. We used to know them all by name. They slept in the barn at the Bochel, but Dad made sure they gave up pipe and matches overnight in case they set the hay or straw on fire.

Some of them had a horse and cart. A family of tinks regularly stayed in the woodie below Woodend. The field of potatoes near them would shrink in the drill. They used to fill a bucket to cook for dinner but no one minded, and they lit a fire for cooking – nobody worried about it spreading. Tinks used to come into the kitchen to make tea in a tin can with a handle to hang on the crook. They loved a strong brew. One of the wives had a baby, so of course the doctor and nurse had to attend her right there. She had an older boy, and Mam said he should be at school. His mother replied that she thought he would be better with another summer among the flies.

When the tinks called at the door they would ask for a drink of water, but usually we gave food as well. Then when she was leaving the woman would say, 'May God bless you and give you the glory and happiness of Heaven.' I think they must have got Social Security later on as they just stopped coming. We really missed them.

The boarded-out children started in the 1920s when the first family came from Dundee. They were the Rileys – Molly, Jim and Henry. It was sad how they often separated the families. Henry was away over on Blyeside while Molly and Jim were at Woodside Cottage. Jim was very clever at drawing – I used to get him to do mine at school as I couldn't draw a straight line. I think the Glasgow ones came next. Quite a few families took children from Edinburgh, but some preferred the Glasgow ones because they got better clothes.

Glasgow paid eight shillings and sixpence a week for each child and Edinburgh nine shillings. The money came through every six weeks by a cheque to be cashed at the Shop. The shopkeeper was pleased as it helped his sale of groceries. My uncle Charles Stuart had given up the shop because trade started to go down, so the boarded-out children were a great boost. Glasgow boys left school at fourteen, then went back to the city and were taught a trade, but the Edinburgh ones were encouraged to stay and work on the farms. Of course some wanted back to Edinburgh, especially the girls, to find their families. I thought it was a pity that boarded-out children who were clever at school never had a chance of further education, but the same could be said of the local children.

Our Mam took in a family of five Emmett children after Canon Stuart wrote to her from Edinburgh saying that their mother was dying in hospital. She had a still-born baby and took milk fever. The mother didn't want any of her sisters to have them as they weren't Catholics. She herself was a convert. Her husband had been drowned at sea a few months before, and she asked Canon Stuart to find a good Catholic home for them. It was quite an undertaking for us at Comelybank because our only drinking water was from a pump. Of course there was plenty clean water in the burn for washing. John Emmett wrote to me a while ago from Brampton near Toronto:

> I was barely six years old when I lost my father and mother. I remember the long trip to the Braes with nothing to eat until we reached the Braes. This woman Miss McKay kept telling us to sit up straight all the time we were on the train. It was not a pleasant trip. We arrived at Comelybank very scared and lonely, until this beautiful lady, your mother, and you, Meggie and Mary made us very welcome and part of the family. Yes, your Canon Stuart sure did a wonderful thing for the Emmett family. I cannot remember your mother ever raising her voice to scold us. She always had good words for everyone and was a saintly woman. I have a lot to be thankful for, being brought up by

your mother and taught by these two wonderful teachers the Hornbys. They gave me the backbone to make something of myself.'

Miss McKay was in charge of boarded-out children. She came up and left a red book with all instructions, saying that if any of the parents called we were to inform the Home straight away. Mam always waited until after they had gone back to Edinburgh. Parents went to their public library and found out the most Catholic part of Scotland, Glenlivet. Two aunts once came to the school and took the children away because they weren't happy about where they were staying. Some parents walked all the way from Edinburgh, sleeping in barns. They slept on straw in the barn at the Bochel. One little girl aged five remembered her mother running after the train crying as it left Edinburgh. The parents came up later, and the girl was so like her mother. Later I met her in Edinburgh dressed in an ATS uniform. She recognised me and was all smiles.

Some of them came back as adults to see the families that had taken them in. Our mother had around twenty children in her care over the years, and plenty of them returned, to Millbank as well as the Bochel. One boy called Frankie Traynor went back to Edinburgh when his mother got married. He was only six years old at the time, but I gave him our address on a label. Frankie carried it all through the years and came back to see us after he married. He brought his wife and children, and later on he even travelled up for Mam's funeral. A Jesuit priest who was giving a mission at Chapeltown went round the houses and often noticed that the lady of the house wasn't the mother of the child running around. He said in Church that all of these women would go to Heaven, as they gave these children the same love and care they had given their own, and brought them up in a family home instead of leaving them in orphanages.

The evacuees were another lot of new children who suddenly appeared in the Braes school during the Second World War –

in fact they arrived the day before war was declared. I came back to Glenlivet myself at that time from where I was working in the south. The train had only dim blue lights on and it was a bit dreary, but I was glad to be going home to the Braes and freedom.

There was great excitement sorting out the evacuees in the School – it was a fiasco, with children labelled where they had come from instead of where they were going. Each mother had two or three children under five, and these ones should have gone to a hostel in Aviemore where the women could have done their own cooking. You can never have two women in one kitchen. We were meant to get children on their own. If we had, they would have settled down, but in a fortnight all the women wanted home – they wandered up and down the roadside at Chapeltown looking for a fish and chip shop.

Two sisters who both had children were deaf and dumb, so Father Murdoch took them in. Everyone who passed was amused to see nappies on the line at the Chapel-house! He got them into a house at Bankhead, but then they quarrelled. One got locked out by the other, and she landed back at his door to complain – in sign language! He had to go over and read the riot act.

Another woman who was staying at Auchavaich got drunk and was found lying at the back of the Shop, so a man was sent to yoke the horse and cart and take her home. He put some straw in the cart to give her a soft seat. All the mothers seemed to be on Social Security. A man came with their money, and they had to pay so much for their keep. One wife said if she helped in the house she shouldn't have to pay over any money, but she didn't really want to work. Some of the husbands came up to see them, and then away they all went home. I heard from my cousin May that those who went to Braemar didn't appreciate the scenery, and they were last seen at the bus stop for Aberdeen on their way back to Edinburgh. It wasn't easy for anyone, and these city folks didn't really fit in to our way of life, but having the evacuees took thoughts of war from everyone's mind and caused a bit of excitement.

There was a prisoner-of-war camp at Banff with Italians in it, and they came up on a lorry every weekday to cut down trees in Tamvoan Wood for mining props. Whenever it rained they downed tools and went into the hut to make coffee. Father Murdoch thought they would be hungry, although they were given sandwiches. Of course he could speak Italian because he had spent years in Rome training to be a priest, and he used to go over and talk to them. He went to Easterton farm and offered to pay for a bag of potatoes so that they could boil them in the hut, but Mr Matheson gladly gave him some and refused the money.

If the Italian boys were well behaved they were allowed to live out round the farms, and we had one at the Bochel. My sister was at home and she cooked him plenty macaroni. He used to help us in the harvest field on his way back from work. The prisoners always made us taste their tea before they drank it. I think they must have been told that we might try to poison them because they were the enemy. We had to laugh. I heard that at Sir Alec Douglas Home's house in Kinross (he was the one who became Prime Minister) the cook used to have an Italian prisoner-of-war visiting her in the kitchen. He said, 'Don't report him. I would miss my opera every night.' The

young man used to go singing down the road.

Mam had a letter returned from the censor when she wrote to John Emmett in Changi Prison Camp because she said she hoped they were being as well treated as our Italian prisoners in the Braes. John was taken from Changi to Formosa on one of the hell ships and spent three and a half years at a copper-mining camp called Kinkasaski. When the Americans liberated them at the end of the war he weighed seventy-two pounds. Our prisoners-of-war were delighted when Italy came over to our side late on in the war. I remember how proud they were when they were first allowed to walk down the road on their own. They went around the back of the farms, found a piece of bicycle at one place, then another somewhere else, and got a bicycle going along the road. Of course the Italians who lived on the farms were all Catholics, and they came to Mass on Sundays in the Braes Church.

10

·

Church

·

The Church used to be so crowded on Sundays that unless you were early you didn't get a seat. Sad to say, only the funerals of old parishioners seem to fill it nowadays. Every 11 o'clock Mass on Sunday had the same opening hymn:

> Come Holy Ghost send down those beams,
> Which sweetly flow in silent streams
> From thy bright throne above.

They were lovely words but we got so tired of it. It was the same at Tombae, where every Sunday they sang 'Oh Jesus Christ, remember, when thou shalt come again.' I've been told that the wooden seats and pews are really good quality at Chapeltown, but I also remember them being most uncomfortable for children. It was so crowded at the main Sunday Mass that the boys and young men stood around at the back. At one time the sermon was at the end so that if mothers had to rush home to put on the potatoes to boil they could leave. Some of the young people walked out too, so from then on sermons were always after the Gospel and they couldn't escape.

Benediction on Sunday evening at six o'clock was also very well attended. The Church was beautiful by lamplight, and the priest and congregation knelt before the Blessed Sacrament which was displayed on the candlelit altar in a gold monstrance. I remember the hymn at the end of Benediction. It began:

> O Jesus, God of Light,
> How, in the darkest night,
> Bidest thou here alone,
> Not one before Thy throne?

A stranger who came to Chapeltown one Sunday asked Mr Hornby for the words and music, but he refused as he wanted it kept for the Braes. I thought that was rather mean, but he was very proud of his choir. Another lovely hymn began:

> O Virgin Mother, Lady of good counsel,
> The sweetest picture artist ever drew,
> In all my doubts I fly to thee for guidance.
> O Mother tell me what am I to do?
>
> This life alas is often sad and weary,
> And cheating shadows hide the truth from view.
> When I am so perplexed and weary,
> O Mother, tell me what am I to do?

We enjoyed the Missions we had at Chapeltown during Lent, with the Church packed every night of the week and great sermons. At one of them the men were asked to bring down the organ from the gallery with ropes because the priest who had come to give the Mission wanted everyone to sing. He walked up and down the aisle rousing the people, and the organ never went upstairs again. Sad to say, the choir loft hasn't been used for forty years or more.

Every family had their own place and paid seat rent. Sometimes people only had half a seat in the pew because there were not enough seats for all the houses. Some people would go to the early Mass at nine o'clock. Comelybank shared with Tomnareave – the McGillivrays, before they went into the farm of Achnascraw. A little card was inserted in a brass holder at the end of each pew for names. It was just like the Church of

Scotland, and the men who helped the Priest were called Elders. They got a dinner in the Chapel-house at Christmas. Miss McDonald, a Highland housekeeper for Father McHardy, was a great cook. The altar boys had a tea party there too.

Our mother remembered when the Church was opened – the School was used for services while it was being built. They held one penny concerts to help pay for it. One man sang 'Why left I my hame', and he was such a bad singer people said, 'It's a pity he ever left it!' The Braes Church was built with money from all over Scotland. Father Mackenzie wrote to lots of people asking for donations and the money rolled in. Of course everyone prayed to Our Lady of Perpetual Succour which is the name of the church.

> Yesterday the foundation stone was laid of a new Catholic chapel for the wide district known as the Braes of Glenlivet. It is a wild, romantic country far from railways and coaches, but there is a considerable population, and they mostly belong to the Roman Catholic faith. The erection of the new church is due to the energy of the present clergyman, Father Mackenzie. Being close to the graveyard, and built on clayey soil, the old church, which has been pulled down, was considered very damp, and this was mainly responsible for Father Mackenzie's decision to replace it by a new structure. The new church, which is being built to plans prepared by the architect to the Marquis of Bute, will be built in the same direction, but about eight feet nearer the Crombie stream than was the old chapel.
>
> *Banffshire Advertiser*, 24th June, 1896

Several marriages took place as the young girls met the workmen at the building and painting of the Church. A Mr Copland married locally, and of course his son became Monsignor Copland, who is Vicar General for the Aberdeen Diocese. He is at St Thomas's at Keith, which is also beautiful nowadays, with its restored copper dome and lovely fresh colours inside. When the new Church was built at Chapeltown, the Stations of the Cross were all donated by parishioners or their friends in memory of people, with a brass plate under each one. I read them all one day. One was a for man killed in an accident in Skye. Mary Stuart, who lived at Comelybank after her marriage, went in and cleaned them every week. The statues were all paid for by parishioners. The Church floor was scrubbed once a year. Mam got ten shillings for it, and my sisters and I helped her along with some other girls. We used to lift up the straw matting which was laid in the aisle and take it outside to beat with canes up and down the avenue. Nowadays Bill and Irene Grant keep the Church in good order, and at the 1997 centenary the parish council put a new carpet in the aisle. A new altar made by the Father Colin Stewart, the parish priest who lives in Tomintoul, was also installed.

The opening ceremony at Chapeltown took place at eleven o'clock on Wednesday, when there could be seen from out of almost every house in the district little groups of people hastening to the church. At the entrance to the short avenue leading to the church there was erected a massive arch of evergreens, red rowans and heather bloom. The arch was surmounted by a cross, and beneath was the word 'Welcome' wrought with ivy leaves on a white background. Over the arch on either side there floated flags, and colours were also displayed from the tops of some of the little clump of trees that separate the church from the roadway.

The outside of the building is plain, with its arched doorway and small windows of miniature panes of glass, as if to retain as much as possible remembrance of the antiquity of the place. Above the doorway in a small recess in the wall is a representation of the Virgin Mary, 'Our Lady of Perpetual Succour', to whom the church is dedicated. The image is of white material and serves as a most beautiful and appropriate relief to the front gable of the building.

Banffshire Journal, 11th September, 1897

The statue above the outside door is actually Our Lady of Lourdes, but there is a picture of Our Lady of Perpetual Succour above the altar with St Bernard and St Alphonsus on each side. The statue of Our Lady of Lourdes which used to be in the Church was moved to the school in Father MacWilliam's

time, as we already had the same statue outside the front door. The one there now was on a wooden stand by the staircase to the choir gallery. It was white – I think it was spoiled by whoever painted it bright blue. St Joseph was to the left of the altar in my day, and the Sacred Heart statue used to be at the back of the Church, according to Mam. She said that there were hearts on the wall there, but they were painted over before my time. The Sacred Heart statue has always been where it is now. As anyone can see, Chapeltown is by far the most beautiful of the three compared with Tombae and Tomintoul. The stencilling is lovely on the walls, which have never needed redecorating.

The main part of the church is sixty-four feet long and is fitted up with seating for about three hundred people, exclusive of the gallery. When all the candles were burning the scene was most brilliant, the rich carving and the bright colours making it a most beautiful spectacle and one of rare architectural excellence and design. Immediately outside the chancel, with its bishop's chair of carved black oak with velvet cushion, and on the east side of the building is a handsome pulpit, also of carved oak. It rests on a foundation of carved Elgin sandstone two feet high. In the western part of the building is the vestry, from which access can be had either to the chancel or to the body of the church. From the roof are suspended a number of brass lamps on chains of brass, and altogether the interior of the church combines comfort and beauty and everything that is in any way intended to stimulate an interest in church life and church work.

There was a very large attendance at the opening ceremony, the church being completely packed. There were nineteen clergymen present, headed by the Most Rev. Angus Macdonald Archbishop of St Andrews and Edinburgh, who celebrated Pontifical High Mass, and his brother the Right Rev. Hugh Macdonald CSSR Bishop of Aberdeen, who preached the sermon.

At Christmas 1939, in the first year of the war, parishioners were told that no Midnight Mass would be possible at Chapeltown because the windows in the Church were not blacked out. However Val Kilbride asked a few other men to find a tall ladder, as the windows are very high, and they got it done – every window blacked out. Word got round that they could have Midnight Mass after all – news travels fast in the Braes. The other two churches had not blacked out theirs, so more people came. Father MacWilliam wasn't expecting many for Midnight Mass at Christmas 1946. It had been snowing and then a thaw came with the rain. It was raining buckets and he thought no one would come, but he didn't know us hardy folk. The brae down from the Bochel was like a river, so we put on wellingtons and waterproofs and set off through the fields to escape the raging torrent, then changed into dry stockings and shoes in the porch at Chapeltown. The Church was packed. Towards the end Father MacWilliam ran out of communion bread and about ten people had to turn back.

One of them was a Mr Gallacher from Glasgow who was visiting his mother-in-law at Broombank. Her husband had died and she was living alone. He only had the suit with him that he was wearing, so when he got home through the deluge he left it to dry all night by the living-room fire. Father MacWilliam went up to Broombank on Christmas morning to apologise for not being able to give him communion. He chatted with the old lady for a long time but Mr Gallacher never appeared. Her memory was going and she didn't realise he was needing his trousers. Meanwhile he was waiting for her to bring them to the bedroom. In the end the priest went back to his Chapel-house, and Mr Gallacher went down later to explain why he had not come through. They had to laugh about it! Father MacWilliam left after only three years at Chapeltown because Bishop Matheson wanted him in Aberdeen as his secretary.

A highly successful concert was held at Chapeltown Hall on Thursday 14th August, 1947 in aid of the church decoration fund. Father MacWilliam, parish priest, was the organising genius and the effort was patronised by the R.C. Bishop-elect of Aberdeen, Dr Matheson of St Mary's, Dufftown. Foremost among a group of talented artistes was Mr James Crampsie, who occupies an important post in the Scottish section of the BBC as Director of Drama. His witty and original sketches brought prolonged applause. Songs were rendered by Father Rogers of Glasgow, Mrs Stuart, Mr Geo. Gordon, Nurse Matheson and Mr O'Connor. There were items by the Braes boys' choir, while sketches, recitations and monologues were given by Mr Robt. Lamb, Mrs L. Shaw and Miss Mollie Grant. Mr Duane proposed a vote of thanks to the organisers, the artistes and the able accompanist, Mr Gaffney.

Father MacWilliam was disappointed to leave the Braes. He started the Scalan Association and became really interested in history while he was at Chapeltown. He had a tablet erected in the porch to commemorate Abbé Paul McPherson, who built the original church, on the centenary of his death in 1946. Father Phillips, who followed Father MacWilliam, belonged to Braemar and was a relative of the Beatties – Jessie Robb's family. He used to say in his sermon on the Curé d'Ars, 'I am just like him, a plain country man'.

Father Shaw was at Chapeltown when I was a girl. He was a great gardener and never had a weed in the avenue. There was a grand vegetable garden at the back, beside the graveyard, and he planted the lovely rhododendron bushes in front of the Church that still bloom every year, pink and white. There used to be myrrh growing there as well which had a lovely smell, and as children we would pick it and suck the stalks. One Sunday Father Shaw announced that he didn't like the girls coming to Church in V-necks and flesh-coloured stockings, which was the fashion in the 1920s – he should have seen the fashions now! The following Sunday they were all in black stockings or else dark brown. Father Shaw started the Children of Mary. He also persuaded every house in the Braes to buy a Sacred Heart picture, either family-size or else smaller for a single person. Families filled in the names and he had them all framed in gold, then came to the house and blessed them with some prayers. I saw one above the mantelpiece at Culantuim when I walked up from Calier recently. The house was full of old furniture and the floorboards were rotting away but Father Shaw's Sacred Heart picture was still hanging there.

The last priest to live at Chapeltown was Father McCabe. When he came to the Chapel-house he thought he would like to cast some peats. Every farm had its own moss, and Father McCabe was told where his was. A man who used to come and do odd jobs was asked to wheel out the peats. He was quite elderly, and when he had his supper and pay he said, 'Weel, if you get as much heat out of the peats as I've had rowing them you'll do gey weel.' He was sweating at the job. We used to call him 'Weary Willie'. Men working on the Priest's fields used to come in to the kitchen through the milk-house for their meals. Father McCabe had two big trees cut down as he thought they could have crashed on to the Church in a gale. There used to be a gate leading round to the front garden of the Priest's house. No one ever went to the front door, though. The gates with their great pillars were put on in Father McCabe's time. Robbie Lamb said they were like Barlinnie Prison, but they kept sheep out of the avenue. When Father McCabe was taken from Chapeltown by the Bishop in 1961, Robbie said 'It should have been the last light to be snuffed out, not the first.' I suppose he was thinking of Scalan.

Before people had cars to get them to Church, the bell was rung half an hour before 11 o'clock Sunday Mass to let them know to leave in good time, either walking or on bicycles. They stopped having Mass in the Braes every Sunday in Father Skelly's time – that was in the 1970s. He had to drive round from Tomintoul, and was getting quite old. Someone suggested that saying three Masses on a Sunday at Tomintoul, Chapeltown and Tombae was too much for him, but he never complained. Nowadays Father Stewart, who is much younger, takes in Aberlour and Dufftown as well. Sunday Mass is one week Tomintoul, one week Tombae and one week Chapeltown. Father Stuart has a four-wheel drive, and one Christmas he arrived at Tombae for Midnight Mass to find nobody there. Snow was so thick on all the side roads that no one else could get through. Most people have cars nowadays and give lifts to those who don't, but Sandy Matheson still comes down on his bike through ruts and puddles from Scalan.

11

.

Scalan

.

You can see Scalan was once a great place with its two water wheels and all the different buildings. Of course a long time ago it was where boys came to learn Latin and other subjects so that they could be priests. Nowadays there's a notice board saying 'The Old College of Scalan', and the building has been restored inside and out. It's quite an attraction for visitors.

Various families lived around the Scalan – McPhersons, Lambs, McGregors, Sharps and Mathesons. I remember Sandy's uncles Fred and Willie Matheson.

> News of the death of Mr Wm. Matheson, Scalan, on 25th June, 1944, caused feelings of deep regret throughout the district. Mr Matheson had attended the morning service at church and on his way home called at a neighbour's house, when he suddenly died. The deceased was born at Scalan and had resided all his life there. On the death of his father nearly fifty years ago he became tenant, and during his long tenancy proved himself a most industrious and capable farmer. Lately he also became tenant of the Old College of Scalan. This historic building still attracts many visitors yearly, so that Mr Matheson was well known to many from a wide area. He was of a quiet, unassuming disposition, a kindly and obliging neighbour, and exceedingly popular throughout the district. He was 74 years of age and unmarried, and is survived by four brothers and four sisters.

It was Willie McGregor Stuart who had the Scalan farm and lived in the Old College. He belonged to Ladderfoot and was the brother of Jeems who lived beside us at Crombie Cottage. When he lived at the College we often used to visit him. Sandy Matheson is the only one left now of the crowd who once lived up at the Scalan. He had two uncles there, Fred and Willie Matheson, and Alex Stuart Eskemulloch was another uncle.

Willie's mother Sophia was a McGregor who grew up at Scalan and married a Stuart of Ladderfoot. She was a great Catholic and brought up her family so well. On Sundays she always came to Church half an hour before eleven o'clock Mass to pray. On Good Friday in those days some of the people, including her, went in at twelve thirty, three hours before the afternoon service began. When she became frail she was taken to stay at Crombie Cottage. I can remember her coming down from Ladderfoot in the horse and cart, with straw for a softer seat. Sandy's granny, Barbara Stuart, married a Matheson and became mother to sixteen children in the house where Sandy is now, to the right of the College building. Of course they weren't all living there at the same time. I remember Mrs Matheson well, a lovely lady. Towards the end of her life her memory was going, and she used to go outside and call Sandy to come down from the tree. He wasn't there, but I expect he did climb it as a boy.

Sophia was adored by her family and she continued to influence them through life. Jeems used to kneel down at his bedside every night to say his prayers when he was an old man in his seventies. Three sons went to Canada and never returned, but their families have been back over since, visiting cousins. Lots went abroad in those days, then got married and couldn't manage the fare home. Most of them kept up a correspondence, though, especially at Christmas time, and sent photos. When they died the family would send the cutting from their Canadian papers with 'Fortified by the Rites of the Holy Church'.

When Willie retired he lived at Rosebrae across from Comelybank. He wore a Homburg felt hat, green with age. Jeems also wore a felt hat. Willie was a bachelor and had a housekeeper when he was at the Scalan. He never went on holiday, saved all his money, and left it to the Bishop's discretion how it was to be spent. Bishop Matheson's father John Matheson was one of the sixteen who grew up at Scalan. He was priest at Dufftown when they chose him, but he wasn't strong and died during an operation for ulcers. All the priests were so upset because he was one of them and he knew the country parishes.

Thanks to Willie McGregor Stuart's money, Nazareth House

got wall-to-wall carpeting. When he had the Scalan farm and lived at the College I used to call there for tea. He once went to Blairs College (a much bigger place near Aberdeen for Church students, just like Scalan used to be) and announced himself to all the clergy professors there as the Rector of Scalan. They were quite amused – they knew the place well from visiting in summer.

Stuck in the Mud

It was a mild and overcast early August afternoon in 1965. Wending down from Scalan to Eskemulloch with a message for Annie, I became vaguely aware of black Angus calves congregated about the gate on Starry Hillock – or was it crows? Nearer approach revealed a priestly posse, some fifteen strong, guessing the spring on Sandy's wee 'humans' gate – the spring-loaded green gate beside the one for vehicles and animals. You could not but note the person of Archbishop James Donald Scanlan of Glasgow, formerly Bishop of Motherwell, of which Cathedral I was a parishioner.

Further down there was a wonderful sight. In the glaur of wet summer a black Mercedes was immovably bogged down. Despite the efforts of sundry clerics, including the Rector of Blairs – shoes and socks discarded and trousers knee-high – the vehicle remained steadfast in the slough of despond. I walked back to Scalan and returned with Sandy and his trusty tractor. This retrieved the situation and vehicle. Back at Scalan, we learned that the party (now a walking party) included Cardinal Theodore Heard, Scots-born but Rome-based, making a farewell visit to his native land. From their respectable 'cairry-oot' Sandy and I were each proffered, in gratitude, a bottle of beer by the neck – spirits being the preserve of prelates.

Later I circled the entries of the Cardinal and the Archbishop in the visitors' book – the former in a thin and frail script (he was an old man, soon to die) and the latter in bold black lettering. After due homage and further convivial confabulation the party departed in high good spirits, two to their rescued limousine and the rest, presumably, to more mundane machines.

John Gallacher (from *Scalan News*, June 1995)

I was there the day Cardinal Heard and the other priests visited the College, sitting in Sandy's house along with my nephew Christopher. The Cardinal was very tall and very old. Did it rain! We waited for a while, but the rain didn't stop so away we went. I've never reached home so quickly – we fairly rushed along through the puddles. Christopher wanted us to go into Eskemulloch but I was so wet I said no. As soon as we were into the house the rain stopped. It was me who got the first visitors' book for Scalan. I suggested it to Father McCabe. It quickly filled up, and there have been quite a few more books filled up since. Sandy used to count the people who came, and there were always between two and three hundred every year.

We never called Willie by the name Stuart. He was always Willie McGregor because he stayed with his Aunt Mary at Calier as a child, and she was a McGregor before she married Sandy McHardy. He loved Calier, and when he retired from Scalan and went to Rosebrae he used to go over there and work. He also delivered the letters twice a week to Glen of Suie in summer because he loved the walk. Willie would never have left Scalan, but the factor refused to give him new outhouses so he just gave up the farm. He hadn't reached retirement age when he left, but had money saved. He wouldn't have received any old age pension till seventy because farmers were self-employed and didn't pay stamps.

Willie went to daily Mass from Rosebrae but only dressed up on Sundays. Most men shaved once a week for Church and didn't get their hair cut very often – in fact it kept them warm in winter. John Stuart Rhindhu was good with hairdresser's clippers. He did a short-back-and-sides for a shilling and a ladies' shingle or semi-shingle, also for a shilling. My sister Meggie, who stayed at Crombie Cottage with her two oldest children during the war, used to love it when Willie visited them in the evening. The girls called him 'Rosebud' because he had a special rosy cup for his nightcap before he left. I always make a point of putting flowers on his grave when I'm back. His stone is quite small, which suits him, because he was a tiny man. I took flowers up to the graveyard one time recently and had to carry water along the road in a bucket from Torview, where I was staying. I always got water from the pump in the Schoolyard but now it's a private house. I have a lovely photo of the school pump with Dominic Gaffney standing by it.

When Fred Matheson had his last illness the doctor came all the way from Ballindalloch by car. Then the drama began:

Car and tractor headlights illuminated the darkness of a field in the Braes of Glenlivet last night as a helicopter from RNAS Lossiemouth flew in to take an 84-year-old man to hospital. Later at Spynie Hospital, Elgin, Mr Fred Matheson was said to be 'very satisfactory'. He had been brought from his home at the College of Scalan, Braes of Glenlivet. The emergency call was sent by Dr Edward Anderson, Ballindalloch, who had called on Mr Matheson from the post office a mile and a half away. Neighbours helped to get Mr Matheson on to a stretcher and carried him to the field where the rendezvous was arranged. Once aboard the rescue helicopter, Mr Matheson (understood to be suffering from pneumonia) was flown to Lossiemouth. Later he was transferred to Spynie Hospital. A spokesman said, 'It is unusual for a helicopter to be used on this sort of mission once darkness has fallen.' Pilot Lt. John Hall (27) said, 'Clouds were beginning to fill in the glen. The conditions were pretty dodgy.'

Fred died a few weeks later in January 1967. That left Sandy on his own in the family house. He cycles down to Chapeltown, or else uses the tractor when there's snow on the grond, and gets a lift

from someone if he has further to go. The post van calls every day with his newspaper. Sandy has always had a dog, of course, to help with the sheep and for company.

George McHardy was brought up in the old Chapel at Scalan – the building on the left opposite Sandy's, which is in ruins now. At one time it was a shoemaker's shop. The thatched roof was leaking at the college end when Henrietta McHardy lived in it. George came back to Glenlivet to walk the hills as a gamekeeper. He had been a hairdresser, first in the USA and then Glasgow. Henrietta, or Rita as she became, brought up the two boys at Scalan when their mother died. She never married, and was the last McHardy at Scalan. When the roof went she decided to move, and came down to live at Rosebrae. George McHardy was good to his aunt and used to perm her white hair. Later on at Nazareth House they called her the Duchess because she was tall and had a good appearance.

Monica and Celia McHardy grew up at the Drovers above Scalan. I used to visit Monica in Ditchling Common near Brighton. Celia her sister married the weaver Val Kilbride. Monica married Bernard Brocklehurst, Val's partner in the weaving shop, but when the war came he had to move. Celia and Monica lived as children at the Drovers and went to the Braes school along with their brothers and sisters. The house belonged to McPhersons originally, and is also known as the Clash of Scalan. It was called the Drovers because of the old drove road for cattle which was the Whisky Road in smuggling times. Their mother was Mary Stuart of the Shop, so needless to say Lena Stuart was first cousin to Monica and Celia. I called on Monica in Wales when I stayed with her other sister, Mary, in Worcester some years ago. She always loved the letters I sent her with news of the Braes.

After the Drovers, the McHardy family went down to Clashnoir Cottage opposite Springlea. Then they left the Braes and went to Fort Augustus, where the father worked on the Abbey farm. Then after that they went to Lord Lovat's farm at Beauly for a year before going to Caldey Island in the Bristol Channel. All these places have Catholic connections – the Church of England monks of Caldey all entered the Roman Catholic Church before the First World War. Celia and Val came back to Glenlivet during the last war for the sake of the children, first to Culantuim, then Tomnalienan because it was a larger house. Mam and I got Culantuim ready for them. I remember they had orange boxes with curtains round them for cupboards. All the houses just had hard wooden chairs to sit on in those days. After some time Celia found she was expecting a baby and wanted to go back south to be with her own doctor. Later still they came back to live at Tombae farmhouse.

Looking up at the Clash of Scalan

In August lots of people in the Braes went up to pick cranberries at the Clash above Scalan. Sandy Matheson always knew when they were ripe. Every house you went to at that time of year had cranberry jam, and you had to have a slice of loaf with their jam – which they always thought was the best. Crowds came from as far as Knockandhu. We also picked them above Ladderfoot. Of course we always took a picnic as we got very hungry and thirsty in the hills. One time the mist came down, so we went to Sharps at Clash of Scalan. We got a nice tea there, and Maggie Sharp played the big horn gramophone for us. I remember the song: 'He will woo his bonny lassie when the kye comes hame.'

12

·

Progress

·

A nephew from Glasgow brought up a crystal set with earphones to the Scalan one time. He wanted to fix it up in the living-room, but Willie wouldn't have the noise of a wireless indoors so he set it up in the loft above the barn. It was the first wireless in Glenlivet – this was in the 1920s – and crowds came to the Scalan to hear it. I remember Lily Matheson took me out to hear it. I donned the earphones and heard a lady talking, then somebody playing the piano – I thought it was wonderful. That must have been the start of Sandy's interest in radios. He learned how to pick up messages from America, and people from all around gave him sets to repair.

Sandy has always been very practical, and people also used to give him their clocks to mend. He refused the offer of electricity when it came to the Braes, but he gets very good television reception on a battery set – small screen but a good picture – which he charges from the water-wheel beside his hen house. Sandy fell and broke his leg on the ice a few years ago, and it was only discovered because he didn't appear at Chapeltown for a funeral. Now the Social Services have supplied him with a phone for emergencies so he can go on living there on his own.

There was great excitement in the Braes when Nurse Mann went for her medal to Buckingham Palace. There were no cars then. Sandy the Mill had a pony and trap so she was taken to Ballindalloch Station, then took the train to London. Later her health broke down, so she came as housekeeper to the School-house. Nurse Mann was Mrs Hornby's sister. She was a lovely person, and it was nice to have a real nurse living in the Braes. Once she gave my sister Meggie a cake to bring home to our mother. The burn was in spate, and as Meggie was gazing into the swollen burn she dropped the cake in. She ran along the bank but couldn't retrieve it. She went home and told Mam about it, who insisted that she went back to thank Nurse Mann for the cake she never saw.

Then cars began to come in. Three women hired one to go to Ballindalloch station for a day's outing by train. It was an old Ford – a wreck, and very noisy, but it always got you there. The driver, Sandy Irvine, would not let his clients miss the train. The car kept breaking down – once he took a hammer to it and got it going again. One of the women Lena Achdregnie lost her raincoat, but she thought it would be in the car. When Sandy arrived back to meet them off the train he was wearing the coat, and it was so black with dirt she didn't ask for it back. They had a good laugh about it when they got home.

Sandy Irvine was very good to children. Whenever we saw his car at the Shop we all jumped in, and if there wasn't room we hung on to the dashboard. He never said 'No more'. He was a cripple – I don't know if it was because of the war. Once my sister Meggie and I found ourselves with four miles still to walk to Aberlour. Were we pleased when his car came along! You could hear it long before it arrived. We reached the shops in Aberlour all the sooner, and had time to look for a penny ice-cream cone or a tuppenny wafer – a slider, we called it. We went from shop to shop to see who would give the best bargain for our pennies.

Walker's Bakery van came up to the Shop on Mondays and Thursdays with bread and cakes. One summer we went over in the empty van to stay at Lyne of Carron with Jessie Bruce who was Jessie Grant Bochel before she married. She was a daughter of Granny Bochel and her husband, a relative of the McHardys of Bolletten, was grieve on the farm. It was all arranged that we would go across there with the van and back after the holidays. On the way back we had a long time to wait by the roadside while the driver loaded his van at the Bakery. We took a seven-pound jar with us and picked raspberries. We managed to fill the jar and made jam when we got home. The driver had to deliver bread and cakes all the way back from Aberlour to the Braes, but we didn't mind how long the journey took. He even went into a shop to buy a bar of chocolate for each of us. The bread which he loaded at Aberlour was still warm when we reached home. The Walker boys were twins. Now Walkers send shortbread all over the world. The driver told us they were the nicest people he ever worked for.

Talking of bread, when Alistair Ladderfoot was a boy, one time he had to carry a loaf home from the Shop. It was done up in tissue paper and tied with string. He was only small, and he got so tired that he undid the string to make it long, and trailed the bread behind him. He was passing Corrunich when they saw him and called him in. You can imagine how dirty the bread was by then, with the paper all torn, so they gave him a fresh one and took his to feed the hens. After he had tea with them, and bread and jam, they sent him on his way refreshed. They probably saved him a thrashing.

When electricity was being put into Banffshire, it went up by the Knockandhu towards Tomintoul, and the Braes were bypassed. This was about the time of the 1965 general election, and the MP Mr Duthie was all for the fishermen in the coast towns. Johnnie Russell suggested the Braes people should write a letter to him about the electricity – he and I wrote it together in the Shop. The letter also pointed out that troughs were being put in some of the fields for the cows, but there was still no running water in the house of a lady who was in her eighties. She had quite a walk to a spring at the bottom of the field near the road. When Mr Duthie came to the Braes Hall he read the letter out. Shortly after that electricity came to the Braes, and water was also brought to that house.

Chapeltown got council houses next to Comelybank when Chivas Regal started up – three for Distillery workers and three for elderly or retired farm workers at Chapeltown. There was also one for the manager and one for the under manager at the Distillery.

> A new £1,000,000 distillery on Speyside was opened yesterday (30 May 1974) on its official handover to Chivas Brothers Ltd. by the Builders John Laing Construction Ltd. In front of the distillery – which has been built on modern lines in natural stone with a pagoda roof – officials took part in a tree-planting ceremony. To be known as 'Braes of Glenlivet', the distillery has a production capacity of 12,000 gallons a week. Although Laing's have a wide experience in brewery building, this is the first distillery they have completed. Mr John Ashworth, managing director of Chivas, said that in bygone days the Braes of Glenlivet area was famous for its illicit stills, and on several occasions troops had to be moved in to put a stop to this practice. 'This is the first distillery in this area since these days – and it is pleasing to think that we have come back in legitimate form.'

The top house at Chapeltown went for £300 when council houses began to be sold – there were never many Distillery workers and it's all push-button nowadays. No fireplaces were put in the houses. It was summer, and no one seems to have told the builders about Glenlivet winters. The Council put in underfloor heating, which is very expensive to use – especially in the Braes. They learned from that, and put fireplaces in the Tomnavoulin council houses. Jessie Robb told me she was very cold with her windows out and the door open while the workmen were putting in double-glazing. She said it was enough to give her double pneumonia. If the electricity breaks down in the Braes, as it quite often does in bad storms when there are power cuts, the people in those houses can't even make a cup of tea, and they have no heating of any kind.

The Distillery have their own arrangements for emergency supplies of electricity, in fact the place is floodlit at night, which looks strange in the middle of the country. The last I heard, Chapeltown was to get street-lighting the same as Tomnavoulin, although normally there has to be a shop for that. Tankers go in and out of the Distillery twenty-four hours a day, and the road is always quickly cleared after snowstorms nowadays. When the water-bottling plant between there and Eskemulloch starts production there will be even more lorries, and there's talk of bringing workers up by bus from Elgin. Just imagine – after all these years of people having to leave in search of work and now coming back in buses! I wonder what Robbie Lamb would have made of it all.

Summer Review of the Braes of Glenlivet

This summer of 1957, which I think has had no equal in fifty years, was unkind to both crops and grass and left us a legacy of green corn which must now be harvested in case an early winter follows on. In spite of cold and wet, the reproduction of wild-life is surprising. With admirable tenacity most wild birds raised a fair number of chicks. Oyster catchers, gulls and curlews seem a little below average, while lapwing and grouse are not so good and partridge poorest of all. Crows, wood pigeon and kindred souls have flourished (the deil's bairns hae the luck o' their faither). Hares are quite numerous, but already over-eating of green corn is killing off large numbers of young brown ones. I cannot say how tame bees have fared, but wild bees seem to be on the point of extermination in this district.

Despite the weather quite a few summer visitors came to the glen. They are indeed welcome for they help to fill the empty spaces and their company is highly appreciated. But nothing is done to make conditions more attractive. The road beyond Chapeltown to Scalan is in a deplorable condition. The bridge of Vataich is merely a collection of loose boards which plays a devil's tattoo as one crosses with a tractor. Beyond Eskemulloch the road deteriorates into a complete quagmire which pilgrims to the old College of Scalan have often to leave and walk through the fields.

Half a century ago the blue peet reek curled from the chimneys of one hundred and twenty dwellings in this glen – from the farms and the crofts which were large enough to keep horses, from the smaller crofts where only one or two cows were kept, from the homes of carpenters, millers, shoemakers, masons and tailors, from the cottages which had only a small garden. Then was the country bubbling with young life, for on many of the holdings were large families of strapping lads and winsome lasses, and church and schools were filled to capacity.

Twenty-five years ago the 'reekin' lums' had shrunk to 76, but with still a fair number of people, and although the smiddy hearth was cold most of the trades were still represented. Today there are only 48 inhabited dwellings in the glen, and a blacksmith comes to Slateford Smithy two days a week. Scanty now is the congregation at church, and few the pupils at school. Some of the dwelling-houses on the uninhabited crofts are still standing, but many are not. The gardens, once the pride of their owners, are grown over with weeds and nettles, with perhaps a stalk of rhubarb and a broken and forlorn rosebush, and the wild pigeon nesting in the trees, while from the roofless ruins an owl hoots to the moon. It is indeed a scene of desolation.

What of the future? I would hazard this opinion. The battle for the glens will be between the Forestry Commission and sporting interests, with perhaps the mass-linked agricultural units as third contenders. Whether they fight or co-operate is immaterial, for the hardy hillside crofter will have vanished forever. There may be prosperity, but with the immortal poet let us say, 'Ill fares the land: to wasting ills a prey, when wealth accumulates – but men decay.'

Robert Lamb

13
.
Places
.

Jessie Robb could remember when there were eleven lights along the row of houses at Larryvarry. Annie Cane and Jean Brodie used to come to one of them in the summer. There are Brodies on a gravestone at the bottom near the cemetery gate. They were both priests' housekeepers and they used to come on holiday to stay with Maggie Sharp when she moved to Greenbank. In later years John and Maggie bought Broombank, above the Church, and gave up the croft at Greenbank.

When we were invited out to tea at someone's house there were always lots of tea leaves at the bottom of the cup – no tea bags in those days. When we went to Daisy Cottage, Jessie read tea leaves (of course she didn't charge) and we believed every word she said about our fortunes. Jessie's mother was even better at it. She spoke Gaelic, seemingly, but Jessie herself only knew a few words. She once said, 'I never liked the Gaelic. I suppose it would be all right if you could understand it'. Jessie had a hard life looking after her mother, then her husband and niece, and finally Bell, her sister, when they were both getting on in years. Their name was Beattie. The family was very poor and only had a very small croft, Newfield in the Carracks, but they managed somehow. Jessie was once teased about a boyfriend she had – this was when she was very young –

and she said, 'He'll have to put a ring on my finger first.' She was proud of her daughter who became a teacher.

The wood above the Church was called the Plantation, and Jean Shaw's house was behind it between Broombank and the Carracks. There was an older house below Fuerandearg where John and Maggie Sharp's parents moved to from the Clash of Scalan. It was near the house which is still standing at Easter Scalan. The one above Broombank was called Greenbank. Stopani Stuart lived at Easter Scalan. He was named after an Italian saint. His parents called him Alexander Stopani Stuart so the initials were ASS. He and his wife had five daughters and one of them, Elsie, is still in the Braes married to Jimmy Stuart. Now they live in the top council house at Chapeltown.

The trees round the Chapeltown graveyard have crows nesting in them nowadays. What a noise they make! There are far too many crows in the Braes. In the old days the gamekeepers would have got rid of them by destroying the nests – much more sensible than shooting them – but now there's only one keeper where there used to be three. Mary and Nancy once went on holiday to the Kirkie and found the place in a terrible mess. A crow had fallen down the chimney and couldn't get out – there was soot everywhere and lamp glass broken. Another time there was a crow's nest in the chimney, and when the men went up a ladder to investigate they wouldn't move it because there were young birds in the nest. They next tried wire netting over the chimney but the crows picked it off and used it for nests. That's why the Kirkie now has whirly things on the chimneys. It was a sister of my great-grandfather who quarrelled with the Priest and started her own church at the Kirkie – so Mam told me.

Mam called her Grandmother Cameron's house above Achnarrow 'Star Cottage', because a tiny flower, very pretty, grew in the woods there. Now it's Woodside Cottage. That's different from Woodend, which is just before the Woodie, that awful blind corner near the Kirkie. Clashnoir Cottage, hidden

now, is among the forestry below Springlea. Johnnie McKay Nether Clashnoir was killed on his bicycle coming down from the Sandy Hole to the bridge below the Kirkie. It's very steep. Some years later, Alex Grant of Auchavaich and Eskemulloch was coming home from a dance. He fell off the bicycle at the same spot and was found in the early hours of the morning. He was carried into the Kirkie house and his sister sent for. Mam and I were cleaning the School when Annie came in crying. She had walked all the way – no cars then. Alex was in a coma for two days and never the same after it.

Nellie Michie had a house at Tomnareave, and she eventually died leaving no will. Her aunt who used to live with her had put money in the bank, but she never touched it. A solicitor came to our house to find out if there were any relatives. Long before that the Michies went to the USA from a house opposite Corrunich, Corrie Demick, which is now more or less a ruin. Her name was advertised in all the American papers, but no one wrote to claim the money. Funeral expenses were taken out of it and a gravestone put up, but the Crown got the rest. Jessie Beattie remembered the aunt carrying Nellie on her back over to Tomnareave when the family left for America.

Robbie, James and Mary Jane moved from Bolleten to retire to Crombie Cottage. When I looked in at Bolletten lately, I thought to myself that Robbie must have had to duck down going in the door there as he was such a tall man. The rooms in the houses were tiny but most of life was spent outdoors working on the farms. Bolleten had lovely yellow roses still blooming in the garden. Everyone had a garden and grew their own vegetables. James (or Jeems) died at Crombie Cottage, and when Robbie and Mary Jane got feeble they moved to an old folks' home. They died within weeks of each other. Mary Jane went first and was buried in the Braes cemetery. Then a few weeks later Robbie died. The funeral went off all right in Church, but when the men tried to lay the coffin in the grave it wasn't long enough. The grave-digger thought Robbie would be the same size as Mary Jane, but he was well over six feet. All they could do was leave the coffin on top and send for him. They all went to the Shop for drinks and came back to finish the job afterwards. Robbie would have been annoyed at the mess that was made of his funeral, as he was very fussy.

Mary Jane told us once she didn't like to see girls riding bicycles. She was sure Our Lady wouldn't have ridden a bicycle. One of the girls replied, 'Perhaps she would if they had been invented then.' Of course ladies didn't wear shorts then – only skirts and dresses.

A little boy wanted a bicycle for Christmas and on Christmas morning there was a tricycle. He said in his prayers, 'Oh God! Don't you know the difference between a bicycle and a tricycle?'

Demick lies at the back of Tomvoan wood – its proper name is Demickmore. The house is empty now, but you can see from

the outbuildings and the remains of a water-wheel that it was a good farm. The Stuarts moved to Comelybank from there when they retired, after we went to the Bochel. Charles Stuart Demick's brother was Canon Stuart of the Cathedral in Edinburgh. He was greatly loved by Protestants as well as Catholics because he was broad-minded. Canon Stuart had a bad heart, and he collapsed in the street in 1947. He had just celebrated his Silver Jubilee – twenty-five years a priest – and was up on one of his holiday visits staying in the Chapel-house not long before. He had a motor bike to take him about as his heart wasn't up to much walking.

There was a path marked by large poles at the top of the Carracks which the people used when they were coming over to Chapeltown. It was called the Ceylon Road because of a man up there who had once worked in Ceylon. The path went on down to the Backside of the Braes opposite Calier. It was much nearer than walking round the road by Clashnoir. There used to be a bridge across the burn at Calier. It's gone now, but you can still get over by using the fence which crosses it to keep cows from going into other fields. Robertson the keeper's cottage was just above the Slateford Smiddy.

The next farm to Calier was Lettoch, where they used to give the workers a clootie dumpling and cream at Cliack. That was when all the corn was cut. There was also a Harvest Home when the corn was all in ricks around the farm. James Matheson and his sister Henrietta finally retired from there in the 1950s and went to live in Aberdeen.

Lettoch Sale

On Thursday all roads in the upper district of Banffshire led to Lettoch for the displenish sale of implements and furniture and the dispersal sale of livestock. Over 150 motor cars were parked in good time for the start of the sale, with the local policeman directing the traffic, and one farmer remarked, 'That's the dearest crop that ever steed in that park.' Over 70 cattle and 270 sheep were disposed of, and although thundery showers somewhat marred the day, good prices were realised. The cattle were a superior lot, and cows with calf at foot made up to £55 per head, stirks to £56, and the stock bull £200, while ewes with single lambs made up to £5 14s per head.

A displenish sale is one of the greatest attractions of the farming world and prospective buyers come from a wide area, while non-farming spectators and bargain hunters swell the throng. People meet who have not met for years, and there are many happy reunions 'ower a dram'. Pride and pathos go hand in hand at a displenish roup. There is the disposer's pride in his stock, stock which have sometimes been bred and perfected by the same family for generations. Yet there is pathos too in seeing the gatherings of the years scattered in an hour at the stroke of the hammer. And also it generally means that another family have gone from farming, as usually on changing farms a farmer moves his stock and plenishing.

The displenish sale at Lettoch was held by James Matheson who has farmed successfully there for 35 years and was previous to that farming in Nether Clashnoir. He and his sister Henrietta Matheson are retiring from farming and going to reside in Aberdeen. They will be missed in the Braes for visitors were always welcome at the Lettoch, and as they were natives of the glen their going leaves a blank.

Robb Lamb

One time there was a meeting at the Pole Inn about the Burns Supper and Robbie Lamb, who used to recite all Burns' poems, was there. Afterwards the publican Jack Shewan drove Robbie and Willie Belno up to the farm at Westerton. After a while he got tired of listening to their talk and left them. Robbie and Willie could have walked the three miles to the Pole, but they thought he was going to come back and drive them back to the Braes. They were so far from home they walked to Tomnavoulin farm two miles away, had their tea there and decided to stay the night on the couch and chairs. Willie's wife Bell thought there had been an accident and didn't go to bed till two hours after midnight. About nine o'clock the following morning her husband appeared. He and Robbie had walked the whole seven miles. There was a public phone box, but Willie said he didn't know how to use it – that was in the days of button A and B.

Mrs Stuart had a late child, and her husband had got out of the way of having babies in the house at Maywood, Tom-navoulin. One lovely sunny day the father Donald Stuart and another man, Sandy Irvine, thought they would go for a walk to the Pole, so she gave them the job of pushing the pram along the road. Off they set. After a few drinks they forgot all about the baby sleeping outside and went home. When he was asked where the baby was Donald said, 'Oh! We forgot all about it!' 'Well,' she replied, 'You'll just go straight back and get him!'

When Mr Dodds ran the Pole there was only one chair, and everyone else just leant on the bar counter. Charlie Postie was always 'chairman' because he lived at Edina next door and finished his work early. He went straight for the chair after his high tea. Mr Dodds kept very strict hours, opening at 5.30 p.m. and closing at 9.30 p.m. He was a good publican and stood for no nonsense. Then Mr Cook took over. He had some money from his farm nearby and improved the place quite a lot. He married a land girl called Madge, who came to him during the war, and after he died she got married again to Jack Shewan, who was Mr Cook's cousin. The two of them ran the Pole for many years, and their son and his wife are there now.

14

.

People

.

A family of McKays packed up and were leaving for Canada, so my uncle let them stay in the shoemaker's shop for a few weeks. There was another little room at the back for a bedroom. I expect their mother cooked on the fire. They had a baby, and also a nice little boy. One day he didn't come to school, and the next day he told the teacher, 'I was away getting my photo taken for my passport.' They were relatives of the McKays Clashnoir. There was no water in the house at Nether Clashnoir then, and ten children grew up in it. Jamie McKay who farmed there put on three jackets when he started ploughing in the fields on a cold day. As the day got a little warmer he took one off and left it at the foot of the field. Then in the afternoon he threw another one off. The third was finally discarded and he ended up in his shirtsleeves. He got the nickname 'Jamie Jackets' from this.

Miss Mollie McKay was a teacher who arrived in the Braes from Bathgate and lodged with us at Comelybank. She was a very good teacher. After the six weeks that students did in these days, at the end of the Craiglockhart training and before their first post, she was awarded the prize. She once asked Sydney Gordon Lagual how he knew something: 'Who told you?' He

was quite young. He said, 'I found it out myself.' Sydney was brilliant (the whole family were clever) but so shy. They led a very sheltered life at Lagual.

After a while she married the postman Charlie Stuart and went to live at Edina next to the Pole, so she became known as Mrs Stuart Edina. After they were married she came up every Sunday with Charlie Postie to visit his mother at Eskemulloch. When we were children and had a sunny day during the summer holidays, we would walk down to her house for tea and then walk home again. Charlie's route took him up past Thain, and every day he found a hen's egg laid well away from the house. He just cracked it open and ate it raw. Some time after he told us that I came upon one there myself, but it was in a pool covered with ice and I couldn't get it out – maddening!

My sister was asked to look after a young girl, Lena Belno, going to her first dance. Alistair Ladderfoot, my sister and the girl walked together to Tombae. When it came to the end of the dance a man wanted to see her home but my sister wouldn't allow it. Alistair was brought over. He took one arm and my sister took the other and they pulled her away and off home five miles away. What a laugh her mother had when told about it! Years later she married the man and they had several children. He was much older, but she said, 'Better to be an old man's darling than a young man's slave.'

Once I asked a girl who lived at Nether Clashnoir if she was coming to the dance on Friday. She said, 'No, you don't need to go to the dances when you've got your man.' How Mam laughed when I told her! One girl, Dolly Rattray, thought she would get a permanent wave so she went all the way to Elgin. We were all anxious to see how she would look with her hair all curly. I was disappointed when I discovered it wasn't really permanent, and that it would grow out. I thought one perm would last a lifetime.

The dances used to be in the Braes School. It was never quite the same when the Hall was built in 1930. Everyone loved Chapeltown. Lux was sprinkled on the floor before the dance to make it slippy. What a scrubbing of the floor there was on a Saturday afterwards! Ian McGillivray's mother, Nellie, and John Belno's mother, Bell, at Achnascraw helped Mam. The froth bubbled round them as they scrubbed on hands and knees. Mam got ten shillings for doing it and she gave Nellie and Bell two and sixpence each. It took all day. They had a big fire in the grate with pots and kettles on it to heat the water. They had tea and bread and jam now and again, and perhaps a plate of soup down at Comelybank when it came to lunch time.

Tom Stuart, who became postmaster at Glenlivet and still lives at the Old Post Office, used to go dancing with his wife Ida before they were married. She was dainty and slim, and in Church she wore a pill-box hat. The two of them were lovely dancers in the School before the Braes Hall was built.

> Local historian Mr Tom Stuart, who started a campaign to rescue the Buidernach burial ground in 1993, has unearthed more facts about its past. Said Mr Stuart, 'The oldest stone mentioned in the last report was 1794, but a friend and I went up with scrubbing brushes and discovered a flat stone with "Here rests the mortal remains of John Gordon late farmer at Clashmore who died 8th May, 1790 aged 83 years." We also discovered my wife's great-grandfather's stone – "John McGregor died at Scalan 4th July, 1880 aged 80 years".'
>
> Until the present Forestry Commission track was made no roads led to the Buidernach, and coffins had to be carried across the fields either from Nether Clashnoir or, on the other side of the hill, from Knockandhu past Achnarrow farm. Four mourners, using what were called handspokes, carried the coffin. As 1936 saw a very warm dry period, the first motor hearse managed to reach the cemetery gates bearing the remains of James Irvine of Portsoy. A week later a hearse again reached the Buidernach with the coffin of William McGillivray, known locally as the 'Aul' Sojer'.

Actually William McGillivray was carried up to the cemetery. I watched from the back of the barn at the Bochel as the funeral procession wound its way round the wood. Before she married Tom, Ida went to Craiglockhart to become a teacher. Jessie her sister never married but looked after their mother. A cousin who grew up with them, Peggy Smith of Woodside Cottage, was very pretty but self-conscious about her protruding teeth. No sooner had she arrived in Edinburgh to start teacher-training than she went to have them fixed at the dental hospital. A boy who was training there fell in love with her, and she hopped off to South Africa with him – never did a day's teaching. Her aunt wasn't pleased at the time.

There was another very pretty girl called Annabel who came

home on holiday from London. She had jet black hair and large saucer eyes. A neighbour, Willie Matheson, thought he would call in on his way from the Shop after he'd got the messages. He sat talking a long time with the girl and her brother, Steppie, who never left them alone together. In the end he said goodnight and went out the door, but purposely left his loaves and other messages on the dresser hoping the brother would go straight to bed. So he waited a little while then tapped on the door hoping she would answer it. But instead it was Steppie who had noticed the messages. He went to the door and said very sharply, 'Here's your loaf.' Willie used to tell the tale himself for a laugh about how he was thwarted.

We used to say, 'Friday flitting, a short sitting'. Jean Pansy Lamb came back from Glasgow and bought Beechgrove at Tomnavoulin. She wanted her brother John to come and be caretaker, so he set off with a cart full of his own furniture. It was a Friday. When he arrived she told him, 'You can use this room but not this one,' and so on – she laid down the law and he didn't like it. He said, 'Right, I'm away back home,' and never even unloaded the cart. All the neighbours were peeping through their curtains – what a laugh they had when he turned back! Later on she brought some Glasgow friends to Tomnavoulin. She had been telling them she had a pond at the back, but when she looked out the window it was gone: 'Someone must have filled it in!' It had only been a puddle in the heather!

An old bachelor was washing the new potatoes at the well when a man came along and said, 'You should get a wife to do that for you.' He thought for a minute and said, 'Aye, but she would eat half the tatties!' A child asked a relative why he had never married and he said he was always looking for the perfect girl. She said, 'And did you not find her?' He said no, because she was always looking for the perfect man. Father Shaw did urge the men to marry from the pulpit, one Sunday, but they took no notice. Someone wrote a poem about a widower who married again as an example to the bachelors.

> Oh good Reverend Father, forgive me my past.
> I'm again gettin' merrit, this time it's the last.
> They say I'm gey auld, but then sir – Oh Hell!
> In matters like that, I'm the best judge masel'.

> A lassie is only the age she reveals.
> A man is just as young as he feels.
> Besides, I've a motive that's worth recognising,
> And when I explain there'll be no criticising.

> There's a surplus o' bachelors in oor little glen,
> A' specimens grand o' eligible men,
> But it just tak's a widower tae mak' them courageous,
> For marriage, they say, is aften contagious.

> Noo aff o' me they micht tak' their cue.
> There'll be some excitement – and a jobbie for you.
> The death rate is rising, the birth rate decreasing.
> Tae alter the fact we must get in position.

> So fix me secure and let me aff cheap.
> The money's hard to get and it's harder to keep.
> Young lads may lauch at me takin' the sample,
> Bit then sir (oh Hell!) they'll tak my example.

> Noo since to you I've my conscience laid bare,
> You'll just say a mass, and breathe a short prayer.
> Think it's good spunk o' us twa gaun thegether.
> I'll wager there's lots wad like tae be taider.

'Taider' means tethered.

One October a few years ago I arrived at Comelybank from London for a holiday. I called in at a neighbour for the keys. I should have been there in daylight but I'd spent a few hours with my brother Charlie in Aberdeen before getting the train to Keith – the Ballindalloch line was closed by then. It was dark when I arrived, and I foolishly let the hired car go. The driver offered to shine the headlights on the gate, but I said I had a torch. Then I found it had gone on in my pocket and the battery was finished. I couldn't even see to open the gate. The outside light was on at Crombie Cottage, so I dumped my case. Louie and Nancy were there, and we had tea.

After a while the neighbour Madge Shewan came down as she guessed I was there, with Comelybank still in darkness. Louie and Nancy came up too bringing a large torch. Madge went in, put on lights all over the house as well as above the front door, and then left. After a short time darkness fell again. The electric meter worked on fifty pence pieces, and the fifty pence was used up almost at once with all the illuminations. However Louie came back and showed me how to work the machine. I put a kettle on for hot water bottles and went upstairs. There was no bed made and I couldn't find sheets, so I wrapped myself in a blanket. I didn't sleep much, as there are funny noises in an old house. However next day I had two fires going, got in plenty old logs and sticks and warmed the place up. My niece and a friend with four little children were coming in a few days, so I had fires on all day and cleaned up the house. Whatever the problems may be, it's always great to be back in the Braes of Glenlivet.

15

.

Life at Larryvarry

.

Ann Lamb

I was born at Larryvarry on 25th February, 1902. The day I was brought into the world there was six foot of snow and the doctor never saw me for six weeks because the roads were all blocked. There were eight of us in the family: Jimmy became a policeman in China and then went to Canada; Janet died aged two or three in Edinburgh; Jane studied cookery at Atholl Crescent in Edinburgh, then married in Canada; Willie became a policeman in Edinburgh and had a son and a daughter; Elizabeth was a housekeeper who married and had four children in Vale of Leven; John was a policeman, married with one son, who retired to Glenlivet; Mary became a nurse, married and had one son. I am the youngest, and spent my working life as a nurse before retiring to Stonehaven.

My mother, Elizabeth McPherson, was born at Burnside of Thain, one of the seven daughters of George and Janet McPherson. Our Aunt Jane, who became Mrs McHardy, lived there for most of her life. George McPherson was born in 1814 and his wife Janet in 1823. He was a stonemason and built his own house at Burnside. He also built a lot of the houses in the Braes along with other masons.

Burnside of Thain sounds very grand but it was just a wee house. The bridge across the burn is still there but the house itself is in ruins. We used to go and see them on Sundays. Aunt Janet had a very good-looking family and she herself was always very tidy. She always seemed to be in black, and wore her hair up and a lace collar all around. The family of Abbé Paul McPherson, up at the Scalan, were related – I passed on a crimping iron to my nephew John one time which was used on the sleeves of his vestments.

My father William Lamb was born at Larryvarry. His mother, Ann Stuart, never married, as his father David Lamb left for Canada before the birth. I think Granny was to follow him and marry out there, but Mother said that she was scared of sailing and never went. My grandfather used to write back, and eventually he told her he was getting married to someone else. There were three children of that marriage, I think – correspondence was poor in those days and the family lost touch with him. She never mourned him but just accepted it.

My grandfather, David Lamb, was a captain in the American Civil War and then after it was over he traded in horses. He's buried in Ohio. I have a photo which shows him as a big man with a beard. My father had a beard too. He grew up tall as well and went down to join the Edinburgh City Police. He and Mother were in Edinburgh while their first four children were born. Then when Janet died he was badly shocked, and they came back to Larryvarry with Jimmy, Jane and Liz.

Granny was still living there in her small thatched cottage. After our house was built she had one end of it to herself and, my, we daren't barge in on her like the bairns do now! Mother would say, 'Better knock on the door before you go in.' She always liked a flower in the wee window, and I've still got some of her old flower jugs. She went around the neighbours' houses and had friends in – she didn't entertain, just lived there. I remember Granny as a great knitter. When Father was home, towards the end of her life, he would lift her out of bed on to a chair. She got a new chaff bed every year, and there were never any bedsores. Mother used to wash her every night and comb her hair into pleats – she had lovely hair – and get

up to her in the night. Finally she died when I was about seven.
She was a marvellous granny – Ann Lamb the same as me.

Father built the house himself with the help of two masons
who lived in the Braes. One of them was his father-in-law,
George McPherson. They had to dig and quarry all the stones,
and in the 1890s there was nothing but wheelbarrows for
carrying them. A joiner who was also the Braes undertaker did
all the woodwork in the parlour. He put in beautiful panelling
which came from Delnabo Lodge near Tomintoul, as it was
being renovated.

The parlour had a lovely fireplace, all green bricks and a
nice fender and fire irons. The bedrooms were so cold in
winter, but we had plenty of blankets because we got some
sheep later. The wool was taken to a man at Tomnavoulin, and
he spun it for us. The roof of the house was corrugated iron
and it was the same on the barn and the byre. There was a hen
house at one end and a large stack of peats, as well as fir for
kindling. All the drinking water had to be carried from a
well, but there were rain barrels at both ends of the house to
collect water for washing. There was this well we used to
go to, away over beside Meg Gordon. She would have been
called the 'howdy', the midwife for the district, and she liked a
dram – oh it was comical! When we got home from school
Mother would say, 'The two pails are empty.' Away we went
and carried back water for this big tub which kept her going all
day.

There was a very nice garden, and a porch for shelter against
the wind which had two doors so you didn't get blown away.
Every bit of land was well fenced, with good gates, as Father
was very handy with a hammer. He carried all the nails and
screws in his jacket pocket. There were about five acres of land,
so we had corn, potatoes and turnips. He used to cut all the
corn with a scythe, then it had to be gathered and put in
sheaves, then stooked and later, when dry, put in a rick. All this
was done by hand with a barrow. There was also a small
threshing mill, turned by hand. I believe it's still lying there –

Jimmy Stuart was up from Falkirk recently and he and Edward Stuart went to Larryvarry.

The straw was fed to the two cows and the corn was taken to the mill to be turned into oatmeal, which had to last you for oatcakes and porridge all year. Our first cow came from Grandfather McPherson at Burnside of Thain. The cow got scared one day and tried to jump a fence. I think it had to be killed. At one time we owned a horse called Jess – I have her brasses still, hanging on my wall.

Father worked at various things and was at the tree planting at Tamvoan and the Buiternach. He loved trees and planted some at Larryvarry, but they were far too near the house. Then he was a water bailiff over at Grantown-on-Spey. Later he joined in a contract to provide peat for Inchrory Lodge, and did that for twenty years. The men stayed in bothies all summer, cutting, stacking, drying and carrying it home. Father also earned money at the deer-stalking and the grouse-shooting, and he was a loader for the people who rented the estate. Some of the guests were very poor shots. The estate people were real kind to him and he was always well dressed with a new suit every year. Mother made his leggings, and he always wore good boots as heather was hard on the leather. He used to walk home some weekends over the hills, but sometimes he came on a pony.

I hated when he was away, as it meant there was lots for us to do, especially when the boys left home and there was only Tess and me. We had to carry water from the well, wash up, and learn to knit and sew. Mother was never fond of outdoor farm work (she was so small and never had any extra weight) but she liked her hens and the two ducks that we kept. I remember her walking about eighteen miles with a cow to a sale at Dufftown when Father was away.

Mother was a real good cook and we were never hungry, as she baked and made butter and cheese and also plenty of jam – especially rhubarb. She baked nearly every day, usually scones or oatcakes. About twice a week she used to make skirly for tea. It was real good with fried tatties left over from dinner-time. We had clootie dumplings quite often, but sometimes there wasn't much fruit in them. The blacksmith made metal swivels so that the pots could be pushed back and forwards over the peat fire. I still have the box iron and the wee polishing one we used for the collars.

We ate all the old hens during the winter as they made good soup. Mother made all our clothes. Empty flour sacks were used for lining trousers – not a scrap of material was lost. We had rag rugs on the floors when they were still flagstones and wood, but later we got linoleum. I remember a sister and brother near us, May and Jamie Stuart, who had only an earthen floor with no wood over it, but they were quite warm and happy. Mother did what she could for them, and I was sent over on Saturdays to clean the fireplace and the windows. Old Jamie insisted I took a ha'penny for my work.

How Mother brought seven of us up with no regular money coming in I'll never know. She was never idle, and did a lot of work on the sewing machine she bought with money she got from the eggs sold at the Shop. The light from paraffin lamps and candles was all we had, so really you got used to doing everything in the half dark. Mother was very thrifty and never in her life spent a penny stupidly, and she taught us the same. She had a hard life, and I never remember her having a holiday, hardly ever any new clothes. We had nice curtains from J. D. Williams, Haberdashers, Manchester, price one and elevenpence ha'penny. There was a willow pattern tea set bought with coupons from a baker who came from Tomintoul, Charlie Spalding. I was the youngest and mostly got my clothes second hand – I hated that.

I remember Father bringing Tess and me wool combinations from Tomintoul. They were thick and had red trimming round the neck and shoulders. They made us itch, and we were so glad when summer came and we could take them off. It was hard to get clothes dry in winter on wooden chairs round the fire, and we had to keep turning them – the same with our boots. There were no shoes in these days. Charlie Stuart made our boots, all hand-sewn but so stiff my heels were always sore with them.

In those days no presents were sent or received as nobody had money to spare. We never got pocket money, and only saved the odd penny when there were visitors. The boys spent their pennies at the Tomintoul Market but I never got to go. I was once at the Pole Market and got rock from a man who knew my father. Mother loved nice soap, and when I was working in Edinburgh I used to buy her Pears soap and a bottle of lavender water. She loved to wear a veil to church on Sunday, and later, when I was working as a nurse, I bought them for her at Jenners in Princes Street.

We never went out at night much when we were young. Our parents encouraged us to read by the light of the paraffin lamp. Father was fond of reading and he had people in Edinburgh who sent him books and magazines. One was *Blackwood's Magazine*, but half the time we didn't know what it was about. Later on I used to sent him *The Bulletin* every week. Neither of them ever read love stories. The evenings were spent talking or arguing about money. There was some gossip with the neighbours, too, and card-playing as odd men came in and played for matches, not money. Jock Sharp would come by with Mary. He was a bit of a poet and wrote for the *Banffshire Journal.* I remember people in all the houses at Larryvarry.

The Braes were very friendly in these days. I well remember the men going out for a hare shoot on the first day of the New Year. You can imagine that the shots weren't very good because of the drams. What a time a time they had with drink and dram! The hares were put into a sled – there was nearly always snow on the ground at that time of year – and taken down to the school playground, and you just helped yourself to a hare. We never had much need of it because Dad shot them himself – we had hare and hare and we would say, 'Not again!'

Mother didn't like rough talk or swearing men, and was a very good Catholic. I never heard of her being at a dance or social.

She saw that we went to Confession and Communion often, and she was very fond of going to Benediction at night when she would wear her best clothes. She loved to put on a good hat or a veil for Church. Jane sent her clothes and hats from the house where she worked in George Square, Edinburgh. The lady used to say, 'Get a box and put in all these clothes!' Oh these lovely clothes that Mother had! When she went to the Church people would say, 'There she goes with another new coat on.'

Mother seldom spoke of her earlier life, but I know she always regretted having to leave her nice home in Edinburgh. At one time she worked in the kitchens at Blairs College, where the students training to be priests ate their porridge from wooden 'caups' or bowls. Later she went to a village in Yorkshire as housekeeper to bachelor relations, and after that she came back to marry my father. John and George McPherson were both doctors down there. Their father had the farm at Tomnalienan, and his wife made special cheese which was sent to Edinburgh to be sold. The cheese money went to educate them at university. She was a Protestant, and walked all the way to Achbreck on Sundays. There were only two other Protestant families in the Braes and both had gamekeepers as fathers – the Kerrs at Clashnoir and the Robertsons in Glen of Suie.

Granny McPherson came down to Burnside from the Glen of Suie and was a fluent speaker of Gaelic. Not a word can I say, but I know the meanings of some of the places. She had forebears who worked at Gordon Castle beside Fochabers, and Mother had a queer story about a relation in service there who was fancied by one of the Duke's sons – maybe that's where the good looks come from! Aunt Meg who lived in Elgin was the grandmother of James Wood, the author of many novels. Aunt Mary at Fochabers was married to a shepherd called McKay, but had no family. She was very small like Mother, and I remember how good-natured she was when she came to us for holidays.

Aunt Jane at Burnside had a son, John McHardy, who went to London and made a fortune in the building trade. He played the fiddle very well as a young man, and he knew Scott Skinner. When Skinner came to visit at Burnside Aunt Jane said to my mother: 'Lizzie, will you ask them for their tea? I'm sick to death of them and their music!' So the parlour was laid out. Both Aunt Jane and Mother had good china, and I still have my grandmother's cup and saucer – a lovely green and blue. Some of John McHardy's money went towards the upkeep of the cemetery at Chapeltown. He paid for the extra land which was bought, and for having dykes built and gates put on. He said to my father, 'Choose where you want to lie and we will make it private.'

I never remember any of us being ill – maybe it was because the doctor charged 7/6 for a visit – so Mother was our doctor. She really was quite good at prescribing for anyone who was sick, and was always being asked to 'dress' the folk who died. She didn't seem to mind doing it. There was a very nice mention of her in the *Banffshire Journal* when she died. When anyone was ill or having a baby Mother went to see them with a jar of blackcurrant jelly. She was a bit of a midwife as well, and the doctor always told them, 'Get Mrs Lamb until I come.' He had to come all the way from Tomintoul on a horse, or from Achbreck in Glenlivet, and when my brother Willie was born Mother didn't see the doctor for weeks as there was a storm and the snow, they said, was six foot high.

Talk about sepsis – there was no sepsis! People were self-taught and they were wonderful. Mother told me once how she dressed the baby's cords (or umbilicus). She washed and boiled old white linen rags, dried them and lit a candle. She then cut a hole in the centre of each square of linen and held it over the hole until it was burning, then blew it out and rolled them all up in a clean towel. That was sterilisation and she didn't know it.

Very few women were in bed long, and all nursed and fed their own babies. No money was given them and the family had to manage as best they could. Still, everyone seemed to live to a good old age. There were no ambulances, and seldom was anyone ever sent to hospital. Needless to say some folk must have suffered a lot. I remember being sent to a house with a message and, oh, the smell was awful and the poor woman in bed. Later on that same smell met me in a ward in Edinburgh Royal Infirmary.

I was never far from home as a child. I was eleven when I first saw the sea. It was a school trip to Lossiemouth and I thought it was wonderful, all that water. I had one doll, and I played with the cat a lot. Tess and I also made rag dolls and played hoosies with bits of broken china. There was a pet hen who had a broken leg, and she used to lay her egg in a corner of the porch if she got in. Sometimes I had to go to the Shop for messages. It was also a post office and had a fine counter covered with fancy things (postcards, brooches and so on), and sold materials for the women to sew their children's clothes.

We mostly ran barefoot in summer. We never went away anywhere – nobody did. I remember going on picnics to the quarry where the stones were dug out, complete with a bottle of milk and a pancake and jam. That was the picnic, never sweets or biscuits. We used to go all the way to the Clash to get cranberries. You went away in the morning and got home about tea-time. Sometimes we had maybe seven pounds each, and then they all had to be cleaned and weighed and made into jam – so good on a scone. In summer Father would bring home hares, rabbits and sometimes venison from Inchrory. These all made good stew. Mother salted butter for winter. When the cows were dry we had to take cocoa with water and ale for our porridge.

The boys used to have to carry peats to the school as very little coal was supplied, but in my day that was given up. That school was so cold, and my seat was half-way across. The headmaster used to stand warming himself all day with his back to the fire. Later another couple, the Hornbys, came, and I believe they were much more sensible. Our coats hung on pegs in the entrance, and if they were wet in the morning, well, you just had to wear them wet to go home. My first teacher was very kind, but inclined to favour the farmers' children. Even so, three years running I got the prize for General Good Conduct – it was always a book. The teacher was very fond of flowers and we had to make up posies of them. They had to be wild flowers, and I used a lot of buttercups which I got from the Crombie burn. I was usually second at that and sometimes first. When I was seven I sang 'Won't you buy my pretty flowers?' at the concert. I had a tussore silk dress with a pink cord – I remember it fine – and my first pair of shoes, which my sister Jane sent from Edinburgh

It was a long day from 8.30 a.m. till 4 p.m., and no school dinners. At dinner-time we were all shut out – told to go and play and eat our pieces, even in winter. I remember the pump being erected in the playground for drinking water. Before that you just went to the burn. When I was about ten we started to get a cup of cocoa. I was the chief cook in the making of it, known as the Cocoa Queen. A girl who later went to Canada helped me. We had a large pot which was hung on a crook by the fire. Lots of the pupils brought milk and cream, so it was really good. We collected all the money, a penny a week, and kept it in a tin. The headmaster bought the cocoa and sugar – we always put in plenty sugar.

I remember the coronation of King George V and Queen Mary. There was a bonfire on the Carracks and we had a day off school. There were games, and then we got an enamel mug with the King and Queen on it. We had tea and buns, and I forget if we got sweets or fruit – no fruit, I think, because the only time in the year we got an orange or an apple was at the school Christmas Party. Mother always used to make herself a cup of tea in my coronation mug – she said it tasted better than the teapot.

We mostly left school at fourteen and of course we had to get work. My first job was as nursemaid for the Minister near Tomintoul. Two daughters were at home, and I had to bath them and look after them. I was also the housemaid, up at six o'clock as it was a large manse to look after. There was the cook and me, plus a man to cut fire-wood and look after the garden and the cow. The Minister was very cheery and didn't mind me being a Catholic. I got to chapel in Tomintoul every second Sunday. I was paid £6 for six months' work, paid at the end so you didn't have much money in your purse. I got a day off every two weeks and cycled home. My first bike cost me two shillings and sixpence, but before that I walked all the way – about nine miles through the hills – then back on Sunday. Mother sometimes gave me two shillings or so if her hens were laying well. She used to walk to the hill of the Lettoch with me, and I had to get back to the Manse before it was dark. Over the years which followed I came back to see her whenever I could.

The death took place at Greenstrath Cottage, Knockandhu, of Elizabeth McPherson, widow of Mr Wm. Lamb, Larryvarry. The deceased lady, who was 88 years of age, was a native of the Braes district and the last surviving member of a family of six daughters of the late Mr and Mrs George McPherson, Burnside of Thain. Mrs Lamb resided for the greater part of her life in the Braes and in her younger days, when district nurses were unheard of, her services were frequently sought in times of sickness. These were always ungrudgingly given, and there would be few houses in the district at which she had not at one time or another rendered assistance. A few years after the death of her husband she went to reside at Knockandhu, and during her last illness had been carefully tended by her youngest daughter, Nurse Lamb.

Looking down on Larryvarry and Fuerandearg

16

The Crofts of Scalan

Ann Dean

The line of crofts above Chapeltown offers a silent and haunting reminder of the families that once lived and worked in the Braes. Soon there will be little left to show where the houses and their strips of land were. There is a terrible poignancy about this row of abandoned crofts, their rowan trees still standing, their stone dykes, so laboriously built from the stones cleared by hand from the strips of land, slowly sinking back under the grass. The land drains, dug down by spade and lined with stones, must now be choked and broken as so much of the land is marshy. Each croft had its own spring, but these are now lost.

The Carrachs, planted over by the Forestry Commission, acts as a solid barrier where a hundred years ago it was criss-crossed by many paths. This was Larryvarry's common grazing for cows, one or two for each croft. Calves were sold to the bigger farms at about a week old. Crofters had neither horses nor sheep, but the farmers pastured their flocks on the hill. Sheep now graze over all the land from Scalan to Calier, leaving only thistles and nettles. Get rid of the sheep for five years and the land would be thick with rowan, birch, sycamore and willow, all self-seeded.

Ann Lamb's old home at Larryvarry is now a ruin. The barn section has a corrugated iron roof and all the gable is intact. The house still boasts a chimney-pot, and there is evidence of a more modern built-in fire at the left end. Unusually, there is a window beside the fire on the right gable wall. Some of the lintels on the windows are of wood – stone lintels were scarce and expensive – and there are traces of lime-plastering. Ann has fond memories of the wooden porch with two doors, one or the other used depending on wind direction – a boon in the blizzards of winter.

At one time there was a lovely garden front and back, she recalls, but now it is just trees and thistles. The trees planted right round the house (too close, as they now threaten the walls) were given to Ann's father after he had completed the job of planting trees on an estate; it is possible that the surprising range of trees in the area stems from this. There are sycamore, ash, wych-elm, rowan, birch, Scots fir, aspen and a huge reclining sallow. Nibbled-down shoots of sallow are everywhere. At the bottom of the croft land is a row of pine and aspen, and between this row and the buildings are traces of the layout of fields. Miss Lamb says they had two cows,

calves, a pig, hens, and four ducks which laid their eggs in rushes in the Moss. After school the children had to find the eggs and drive the ducks home.

How did these families survive? Life must have been hard, as the land, weather and altitude were rarely kind to them. For much of the summer there was work enough at home, but mostly work had to be found away from the crofts. In winter there was herding of sheep, fencing, draining; in spring, ploughing on other people's farms. For certain experts, mole-catching brought in some money. Then there was road making and mending, gamekeeping, forestry and seasonal work on the estates, including peat-cutting for the distilleries. In summer, harvest work on lowland farms fitted in well with the later harvest of the Braes. The crofts of Scalan were slowly abandoned from the 1920s.

J. G. Phillips, in his *Wanderings in the Highlands of Banffshire and Aberdeenshire* (1881), writes of calling in to visit an old friend John Sharp. Remembered as Jock by Ann Lamb, he had a two-acre croft at Larryvarry. Phillips describes him as 'one of those book worms whom nature has dropped for the sole purpose, it would seem, of unlocking her secret wonders and presenting them to the gaze of mankind. He was, as usual, poring over a musty volume but laid it aside as we entered and looked up with a bright, welcoming smile.' It is hard to associate a bookworm engrossed in his reading with any of the houses of Larryvarry as they appear today.

We know so little about the crofts of Scalan and all those other homes on marginal land in the Braes of Glenlivet. Who first broke in the land? Was there excitement and satisfaction in the work? Later on, did people resent seeing the younger generation leaving, usually for good, or were they glad that their children were being given opportunities denied to themselves? What could it have felt like to belong to an ageing population, struggling to keep a croft going? Was there reluctance or relief when the croft was finally abandoned?

People who visit the upper end of the Braes should do so on

foot, in small groups or alone. The Old College of Scalan offers a very particular kind of attraction, but bus-loads – even of pilgrims – are alien to the feeling of the place. Walk up from Eskemulloch. Smell the scent of clover and listen to the curlew and the grouse. Then listen to the sounds of silence: the 'raining' of the aspen leaves, the swarms of insects busy in the rushes. Watch the tortoiseshell butterflies on the thistle heads. Remember the lives that were lived around Scalan and among the ruins of Fuarandearg and Larryvarry. The poet Douglas Young provides a fitting epitaph:

The old lonely way of living. . .

> Peaceful bounty flowing
> Past like the dust blowing,
> That harmony of folks and land is shattered.
> Peat fire and music, candle-light and kindness. . .
> Now they are gone
> And desolate these lovely lonely places.

17

The Place-names of the Braes

Stuart Mitchell

The place-names of Banffshire in general and Glenlivet in particular have been largely neglected by major etymologists such as W. J. Watson (*Celtic Place Names of Scotland*) and A. Watson & E. Allan (*Place Names of Upper Deeside*). Even James McDonald of Huntly came no nearer than the Upper Cabrach and a few Mortlach locations in his *Place Names in Strathbogie*. Although the Transactions of the Banffshire Field Club contain papers on the Celtic place-names of Banffshire by Buckie solicitor John McDonald (1882, 1885), and by Dr John Milne of Aberdeen (1905), they are, unfortunately, not very reliable. In a great many cases their 'name-derivation' is simply the translation of a likely-sounding, often literary, modern Gaelic word which takes no account of the actual location, the early recorded versions of the name or, more seriously, the very nature of Gaelic place-names. Although W. J. Watson pioneered a realistic approach to etymology early this century, such unconsidered translations continue to be offered as the 'meaning' of many place-names. This chapter attempts to give better sense to the place-names of the Braes until such time as the etymology of Upper Banffshire can be researched in depth.

Important elements of the landscape, such as rivers and

hills, were the first to be given names by the earliest settlers of an area – the more prominent the feature, the earlier it was named. Conversely, the smaller or more remote a stream or hill, the later it received a distinct identity. Thus, many major mountains, rivers and lochs have names that are not just pre-Gaelic (9th century) but pre-Pictish. Though often much degraded, these survive to the present day.

Almost every Gaelic place-name started as a simple description of the location. In only a very few cases is a local event (usually martial) and its consequences recalled; even more rarely is a person commemorated. It is not just Pictish and earlier names that have become corrupted, as even Gaelic names have had their original form and intention obscured by phonetic distortion over time. This may have been due to an altered physical aspect of the location, changes in vocabulary, or simply the decline of local Gaelic as it was displaced by English. Thus, the oldest recorded version of a name can give important clues to that original form.

Although Gaelic was still spoken by some Kirkmichael residents in the 1870s, it had probably ceased to be the everyday language of Glenlivet a century earlier, usurped by the tide of English rising up the glens. As a result, from the late 18th century onwards almost all new farms and crofts received English names, with those last few that were Gaelic-based doubtless adopted from long-established area-names. Although Ann Lamb's Granny McPherson and Jessie Robb's Cameron mother were probably the last Gaelic speakers living in the Braes early this century, it is most unlikely that either was Glenlivet-born.

Gaelic place-names tend to be quite simplistic and descriptive. The most common elements are:

achadh, ach – field	*allt* – stream
baile – farmstead	*beag* – small
beinn – mountain	*càrn* – rocky peak or hill-top
cnoc – large hillock	*cnocan* – small hillock
coire – steep mountain glen	*dail* – field, plain or river-haugh
druim – ridge	*eilean* – island or riverside green

innis – meadow or island	*inbhir* – river-mouth, confluence
meall – rounded hill	*moine* – peat moss or morass
mór, mhor – big	*tom* – hill
ban – white, fair	*buidhe* – yellow
dearg – red	*dhu* – black, dark
glas – green (or grey)	*gorm* – blue
liath – grey	*ruadh* – reddish
dabhach, doch – land area (200-400 acres)	

Where early versions of names are quoted, '1761' refers to the William Anderson *Generall Plan of Glenlivet* and '1774' to the Thomas Milne survey. Other dates are for entries in the Invera'an Old Parish Register (OPR), or if marked[†] to denote other documentary sources. 'O.S.' refers to the Ordnance Survey maps, 1869–1976.

In 18th century Upper Banffshire place-names, the terms 'Wester' and 'Easter' are equivalent respectively to 'Upper' and 'Lower', regardless of their actual geographical relationship. While this is usually relative to the flow of the nearest stream, it occasionally denotes difference in elevation. As a result, on an eastward flowing stream there can be the paradox of a 'Wester' that is actually to the east of its 'Easter'. Two such Glenlivet examples are at Auchavaich on the Crombie and Blairfindy on the Livet.

* *Gaelic place-names established after the 1761 'Generall Plan'*
° *Pre-1761 places not on the 'Generall Plan'*

Achbreck	(1761 Achbrake) Speckled or piebald field; from *achadh* – field, and *breac* – speckled. Where the road from Dufftown enters Glenlivet.
Achdregny	(1644 Achdregnie, 1680 Achdrignie) Field of thorns; from *droighneach* – abounding in thorns or sloes. It can be dated to at least as far back as the late

16th century through James Gordon of Achdregnie, a nephew of the John Gordon of Cluny who built Blairfindy Castle and died there in 1586. (See also Achnascraw and Tombae.)

Achnascraw (1680 Achnascrae, 1757[†] Achnascrave, 1761 Achnascra) Field of thin sods; from *sgrath* – thin sod (*sgroth* – thick sod). Adam Gordon of Achnascra was another nephew of John Gordon of Cluny. (See also Achdregny and Tombae.)

Allanreid* Bog-myrtle meadow; from *eilean* – waterside meadow, and *roid* – bog myrtle. If the second element is *reidh* – cleared or level place, the name becomes the rather tautological 'level waterside meadow'.

Alltachoileachan° (Locally 'Allt-a-hoolachan') Burn of the hillocks; from *a' thulaichean* (genitive plural of *tulach*) – hillock (pronounced 'hoolachan'). Thus *a' choileachan* (genitive plural of *coileach*, pronounced 'hoylachan') for 'burn of the (grouse) cocks' is much less likely. The Battle of Glenlivet was fought here in 1594.

Allt na Cartach (1761 Altnacardich Burn) 'Smithy Burn'; from *ceardach* – smithy or forge. Also possible is *cardaidh* – wool-carding. Cartach Bridge is near the Pole Inn at Knockandhu.

Allt na Fanich (1761 Altnahinach, Calier Burn) The O.S. spelling suggests 'burn of the flat place'; from *fainich* – flat place (appropriate around Calier and Tomnalienan). Also possible is *phinneach* (genitive of *pinne*) – peg. However, the 1761 spelling might represent (*na h*) –

eanach – wool or down, while *feannag* – hoodie crow, cannot be excluded.

Allt nan Gamhainn° Burn of the stirks; from *gamhainn* – stirk or year-old calf. A stream just east of Achdregnie that would have provided good grazing for young cattle.

Allt Vattiern° (1761 Letach Burn) Possibly 'Tidy Burn' from *bheitiran* (genitive of *beitiran*) – neat, tidy.

Auchavaich (1680 Achivaich, 1719 Auchvaich) Field of the birch wood; from *achadh na bheitheach* (genitive of *beitheach*) – birchwood. This suggests that there was an ancient birchwood on the banks of the Crombie when these farms were established in the 17th century.

Auchnarrow (1645, 1747 Achnarrow, 1680 Achinnarrow, 1761 Achinarrow) Field of corn; from *achadh nan* – field of, and *arbhar* – standing corn. Although '*bh*' is usually sounded as 'v', a Glen Dee farm name with the same *-arbhar* root is also pronounced '-arrow'.

Avon (Pronounced 'A-an') A pre-Gaelic name from the very earliest phase of settlement that comes from the same Indo-European root, *ab* – river or water, as the Gaelic word *abhain* – river.

Backside Local name for the Tomnalienan-Calier area, which is separated from the Crombie by the Moss of Carrachs. Backside Croft, at the top end of Upper Clashnoir, was established before 1761.

Badeglashan (1761 Bedeglashin) Clump of trees at the small trench; *bad* – clump of trees, (*na*) *claisean* – of the small furrow or trench. A farm on the east bank of the

Crombie that was absorbed into nearby West Auchavaich before 1850. The identity of the furrow is uncertain. (See also Clash of Scalan.)

The Baden   (1761 Badin) Place of clumps or thickets; from *badan* (plural of *bad*) – clumps of trees or thickets; the west bank of the Crombie from Refriesh down to Croftbain. The old track here was the original access to the Braes from Tomnavoulin until the modern road to Knockandhu was built across the Muir of Croftbain in 1842.

Bad Finich*   The jet-black thicket, or possibly 'hoodie-crow thicket'; from *bad* – thicket, and either *finichd* – jet-black, or *feanag* – hoodie crow. The moorland slope west of Knockandhu. (See also Allt na Fanich.)

Badievochel   (1680 Badivochell) The clump of trees at the Bochel; from *bad* – clump of trees, and (*na*) *Bhochel* – genitive of Bochel. (See Bochel.)

Ballindalloch   Farmstead of the haughland; from *baile* – farmstead, and (*na*) *daloch* – haughland, flat riverside ground.

Balnacoul*   Farmstead at the nook; from *cul* – nook, or (at the) back. Above Achdregny and also in Morange, beyond Achbreck.

Bankhead   English, 19–20th century (in Gaelic would have been 'Kinbruach').

Belachnockan   (1761 Belochrokin) 'Broom Hillock'; from *beallaidh* – broom, and *cnocan* (diminutive of *cnoc*) – small hillock. Because it lies near the funeral road to Kirkmichael, *bealach* – pass, is also possible. In Gaelic, *cnocan* is pronounced 'crock-an', hence the 1761 spelling.

Belnoe 'Newtown' (Tomnalienan, Achnascraw); from *baile* with *nuadh* – new.

Blairwick (Kirkmichael) Buck's meadow; from *blar* – meadow and *bhuic* (genitive of *boc*) – roe-buck. On the funeral road from Lettoch to Kirkmichael.

Blye Water (1761 Ladder Burn) Fine or flowering burn; from *blaithe* – fine or flowering. *Blaigh* – portion or fragment, has also been suggested.

The Bochel 'The Herdsman' (of the Braes); from *buachaille* – cow-herd. However, its conical shape suggests that the ultimate root of the name may be *boc* – a swelling (e.g. Buck of the Cabrach).

Bolletten* Juniper farmstead; from *aiteann* – juniper. However, the vowel sound suggests that instead of *baile* the prefix might be *buaile* – cattle-fold, or possibly *poll* – pit or hole.

Bolnaclash* (1761 Boil na Glash) Cattlefold at the hollow; from *buaile* – cattle-fold and *clais* – trench or steep hollow, indicating that this was formerly shealing ground. On the Blye Water at the low ground between the Bochel and Tom a' Voan, near Burnside of Thain.

Braeval* Late 18th century (1839 Braevail). Uncertain. Might be 'hill-slope farmstead'; from *braigh* – hill-slope and *bhaile* (genitive of *baile*). The farm lies on the edge of a hill-spur, so *bhile* – edge, margin, or *bheulaibh* – front, foreside are also possible.

Broombank English, 19–20th century. (In Gaelic might be 'Bellachbruach').

Buiternach (1761 Budernach) Unexplained. May

derive from *buaile* – cattlefold, or *buth* – hut, with perhaps *tearnachd* – safety, security. Other possibilities are *tairneach* – thunder, or *tairnnich* – nail. There was a croft of this name above Nether Clashnoir in 1761.

Burnside English, 19th century. There were Burnsides at Calier, Thain, Auchnarrow and Achnascraw.

Cairn More° The big hill; from *càrn* – cairn or rocky peak and *mor* – big. The peak just east of Scalan (also the name of the Shop).

Calier (Locally 'Cal-eer') Unexplained. The prefix is uncertain, but does not seem to be *cul* – nook. However, the suffix may be *earr* – tail or lowest end, perhaps relative to the hill-spur behind; it cannot be western or westerly which always occur as *an iar* – the west.

Carn na h-Iolaire (1761 Craig na Hilar) 'Eagle's Crag' – though now the haunt only of buzzards; from *iolair* – eagle.

Carn Dulach° The thick hill; from *dumhlaich* – thickness. Another possibility is *duallach* – plaited (i.e. many small streams).

Carn na Glascoill Hill of the green (or grey) wood; from *glas* – green or grey, and *coille* – wood. Hill south east of Suie. (See Glassachoil.)

Carn Scrapech° The rough cairn; from *sgrabach* – rough or rugged. Northern ridge of Carn Mor overlooking West Auchavaich and Corrunach.

Carrachs Boggy or mossy place; from the old Gaelic *currach* – bog, marsh. Related and also appropriate are the modern Gaelic *car* – mossy soft ground; *carrach* – uneven surface; and *carachadh* – moving or stirring. As the final 's' has always been present it may represent the suffix *-as*, denoting its large extent. This forestry plantation was a very large peat moss in 1761.

Chapeltown　English, 19th century. Named for the RC chapel built here in 1829 on land that was previously known as 'the Faevate or Littletown of Eskemulloch'.

Christivoan*　19th century. Unexplained, but as it appears to be based on *moine* – peat-moss, this croft opposite East Auchavaich probably took the name by which this end of the Feith Vatich was known – an 'Allt a' Chriostan' recorded from the Braes was probably in this area. This stream name may derive from *criostal* – crystal, *crosdachg* – fretful or restless, *crios* – belt, or old Gaelic *criosda* – swift, rapid. Neither Allt Criosdaidh in Upper Deeside, nor Allt Chriosdain in Glen Loin, Kirkmichael, have been satisfactorily explained.

Claggan　Round bare hill; from *claigionn* – skull. This name is often given to in-field land or the best field, or to the highest field on a hill slope. Often called Claggan of Tombae.

Clashnoir　(1698 Clashinor, 1761 Clashinore) Grassy furrow or trench; from *clais* – trench or furrow, and *fheòir* (genitive of *feur*) – grass. It is 'Clashnyore' locally, so cannot derive from *oir* – edge, like Kinnoir near Huntly. These, with Clashinore in Strathdon, are the only examples of this type of suffix in the North East.

Clash of Scalan   Furrow at Scalan; from *clais* – trench or furrow. This now abandoned croft at the Braes end of the 'Whisky Road' was established about 1720 on former Lettoch and Calier shealing land above Scalan. Abbé Paul McPherson was born here.

Clinkhard*   English, 19th century. Suggests stony, thin ground. It was one of two 1761 crofts on Gerucruie or 'Dubbietown' (between East Auchavaich and Achnascraw) that have now disappeared. (See Gerucruie.)

Colunduim*   19th century. Back of the knoll; from *cul an* – back of, and *tuim* (genitive of *tom*) – knoll or small hill.

Comelybank   English, 19th century. Pretty bank. House at Chapeltown.

Convene Muir°   Uncertain. Possibly from *coinneamh* – meeting (place), or *conas* – whins. Because it covers the lower slopes below Dog's Cairn, *coin* (plural of *cu*) – dogs, is possible.

Cordregny*   (1761) Thorny corrie, as *corrie droighneach* (see Achdregny). The prefix 'cor-' can also mean 'upper' or 'further back', appropriate here.

Corrie Burn   (O.S. Allt a Choire) This burn rises in a corrie at the back of Carn Ellick (near the Quirn) and runs down to join the Livet at Tomnavoulin. It gave its name to the farms of Easter and Wester Corries of Tomnavoulin.

Corrunich*   (Locally 'Corwanich 1774') Place of rowans; from *caorunn* – rowan, although *caoran* – peat fragment, is possible, with the suffix -*ach* – abounding in. Either there had been many rowan trees here or the name refers to the peaty land. It might also relate to nearby Corry from (*Cor'*)-*uainach* – greenish, or even -*uanach* – lambs. That this was the mid 18th century shealing area for Tomnalienan may account for the modern 'meaning' of Tom a' Voan (qv).

Corry* (of Demick) (1814 Quarries) '1774'; Uncertain. The smooth and gentle eastward slope of Tom a' Voan is quite unlike a corrie in the hills. The name of this now ruined croft may have the same origin as adjoining Corrunich (qv), or might denote its 'upper' relationship to Demick (see Cordregny). Despite 'Quarries', there is no sign of even a limestone quarry nearby.

Crombie Water Winding stream; from *crom* – bent with suffix – *ach*, abounding in.

Crombie Cottage English, 19th century. At Chapeltown.

Cùl Allt Back Burn; from *cùl* – back or nook. Joins the Ladder Burn at Ladderfoot.

Culqhinnich* Possibly 'jet black nook'; from *finichd* – jet black, or 'hoodie crow nook' from *feanag* – hoodie crow. Former farm near Achdregnie. (See Bad Finich and Allt na Fanich.)

Culraggie Burn (1761 Achinarrow Burn) Possibly 'burn of the long back-place'; from *cul* – back-place or nook, and *ruigeach* – stretching. This would be appropriate because it runs down behind Tom Cruinn and the Buiternach from the boggy moorland of the Fae Musach to Knockandhu. Also possible and appropriate is 'Misty Burn'; from *(allt) ceothragach* (pronounced

	'kyoragach') – misty or drizzling, from *ceo* – mist or fog.
Daisy Cottage	English, 19th century. Above Chapeltown on the Carrachs.
Demick	Uncertain. While it is possibly 'pig haugh', from *dail* – haugh or field, and *muic* – pig, the name would have been stressed on the second syllable, not on the first as here. Also, *dail* usually retains its 'l' in the Aberdeenshire – Banffshire highlands.
Demickmore	This was the name for a group of crofts that included Demick, so *mor* here is the collective 'greater' instead of just 'big'.
Drovers	Local name for Clash of Scalan (qv) early this century. The old drove road to the Lecht – now called 'The Whisky Road' – started from here.
Drum Moan°	Moss ridge; from *druim* – ridge; and *moine* – moss or morass. The saddle between The Bochel and Carn Tullich, just above Glack.
Easterton	Easter Auchavaich (see Auchavaich). The Easterton above Tomnavoulin was formerly Easter Corries of Tomnavoulin.
Edina	English, 20th century. Cottage at Auchnarrow.
Eskiemuchkach	Dirty marsh; from *easg* – marsh or ditch, and *mucach* (pronounced 'muchgach') – dirty. A former croft on Demickmore.
Eskemulloch	Top marsh; from *easg* – marsh; and *mulloch* – top.
Fae Vatich°	Tufted marsh; from *féith* – marsh or boggy moorland, and *bhadach* – abounding in tufts (of reeds or sedge). The south-eastern end of the Carrachs Moss. (See Vatich Burn.)

Fae Musach°
Dirty moss; from *féith* – marsh, and *mosach* – dirty or filthy. Source of the Culraggie Burn and of the north-west-flowing Chebit Water.

Fuarandearg*
Red Spring; from *fuaran* – perpetually flowing spring and *dearg* – red (i.e. has a high iron content). Eastern end of Larryvarry.

Gallowhill
English, 19th century (overlooking Blairfindy Castle). This name did not appear until about 1840 when Tomoulin disappeared. Presumably used thus by the 16th century Gordons of Cluny.

Gerucruie
Hard short-heath; from *giorrach* – short heath, and *cruaidh* – hard, firm. The 'hard' element of the name continued in Clinkhard (qv), one of the two croft yards here in 1761. Lying between Achnascraw and East Auchavaich, it was identified on the plan as Gerucruie or 'Dubbietown'.

The Glachan°
The little hollow; the diminutive of *glac* – hollow or defile. A shallow saddle between Tom Cruinn and Scorranclach.

Glack
Valley or hollow (of the Livet); from *glac*. On the west bank of the Livet opposite Achdregnie.

Glassachoil*
Grey wood; from *glas* – grey-green, and *choille* (genitive of *coile*) – wood (see Carn na Glascoill). *Glas* can mean either grey, green or grey-green. The form of the name suggests as an alternative, 'pasture wood'; from *glasach* – ley land or pasture.

Grayknowe
English, 19th century – Grayhillock ('knowe' is the Scots word for hillock). Farm on the Livet near Glassachoil.

Greenbank   English, 20th century. The most westerly croft at Larryvarry.

Greystone   English, 19th century (now called Woodend (qv)).

Hillock   English, 18th century. A 1761 croft at Croftbain, now vanished.

Inverblye   English, 19th century. Anglicised reuse of *inbhir* – infall of one stream into another. Where the Blye flows into the Livet.

Invernahaven*   (Locally 'Invernahoun') Equivalent to 'Meeting of the Waters'; from *inbhir* – confluence of streams, and *na h'abhuinn* – of the streams. Several small burns join the Blye near here.

'The Kirkie'   Former Protestant Chapel of Ease at the roadside above Refriesh, now a private house. It was preceded in the mid 18th century by a Protestant preaching-house and school at Badevochel.

Knochkan (Suie) (1761 Knock in Duilt) Small hillock – *cnocan*. It lies on a small peninsula bounded by the Kymah and Suie Burns and the Little Livet (in 1761 called the Little Kyma – though the O.S. map shows that name on another burn a mile upstream). The 1761 name probably represents *knockan da-allt* – little hillock at two streams.

Knockandhu°   (Recorded from 1736) Small black hillock; from *cnocan* – small hillock, and *dhu* – black, dark. The name of this small farmstead in the angle between the road into the Braes and the Tomintoul road was transferred to the present row of houses when they were established as crofts in the mid 19th century and briefly

	called Duchesstown. Now signposted as Auchnarrow.
Kymah Burn°	Either 'Crooked Burn'; from *caime* – crookedness, or an equivalent 'Steps Burn'; from *ceumnaich* – many steps (i.e. sharp bends). The main headwater of the Livet.
Kynakyle	(1761 Kaynakyle) Wood-end or wood-head; from *ceann* – head or end, and *choille* (genitive of *coille*) – wood. Site of the old RC chapel, predecessor of Tombae, that was washed away in 1829. The 1761 plan shows it at the edge of woodland that stretched downriver towards Tombae. Near Allanreid.
The Ladder	'The Hill-slope'; from *leitir* – a hill-slope. This generic name for the range of hills whose uniformly steep slopes close in the Braes to the east and south is an anglicisation of Letterach (qv), the central hill that overlooks Ladderfoot and Demickmore.
Lachnasharrach*	Foal's slope; from *leacann* – sloping side of a hill, and *searach* – foal or colt. Became Ladderfoot in the late 19th century.
Ladderfoot	English, 19th century. Formerly Lachnasharrach.
Lag Glas*	Grey-green hollow; from *lag* – hollow, and *glas* – grey-green. Although the O.S. map shows this as the name of the broad shallow ridge between the Cartach Burn and the Crombie, it probably applied originally to one or other of the stream-hollows.
Lagual	(1761 Lagavool; locally 'Lagoo-al') Hollow of the cattlefold; from *lag na* –

	hollow of, and *bhuaile* (genitive of *buaile*) – cattlefold.
Larryvarry*	(O.S. 1865 Larach Varry) Uncertain, but may be 'heaped site', from *larach* – site of a former building, and *barrach* – heaped (e.g. with debris). Also possible are *larach mhairi* – Mary's site, or 'heaped slope' from *learg* – sloping face of a hill.
Letterach	Many slopes; from *leitir* – slope, with the suffix *-ach* – abounding in. (See also The Ladder.)
Lettoch	(1680 Letache) This common name is usually derived from *leth davach* – half davoch or daugh, but can also be *leth taobh* – half side of a valley, which is more appropriate here.
Littletown	English, 19th century. 'The Faevate or Littletown of Eskemulloch' became Chapeltown after the RC Chapel was built there in 1829. Faevate is 'drowned marsh' (i.e. prone to flooding), from *feith* – 'marsh' and *bhaite* – drowned, submerged.
Livet	(Locally 'Leevat') Nicolaisen suggests 'full of water, flooding'. Probably pre-Gaelic as a river such as this would have been named very early. Milne's suggestion of *liomhaidh* – shining, is unlikely though rather appealing.
Lynavoir°	Big enclosure; from *loinn* – enclosure, with *mhor* – big. Former farm on the upper Conglass Water, Kirkmichael, accessible from Clash of Scalan. The prefix 'lyn-' or 'lyne-' usually refers to an enclosure (often for animals) except in those very few cases where there is a narrow gorge (*linne*) in a nearby stream.

Lynebeg
Small enclosure; from *loinn beag*. (Should properly be *loinn bheg* – pronounced 'Lyneveg'; see Lynavoir.) A farm lying Tomnavoulin.

The Mallens°
('Achnascrave in the Mallens' 1757[†]) Probably the area between the Crombie and the Blye. May derive from *maol* – smooth headland (also round-headed hill), referring to the low rounded spurs of The Bochel and Tom a' Voan which meet at Eskemore.

Millbank
English, 19th century. Beside the Mill of Achnascraw.

Minmore
(1680 Minimore, Minmoir) Big moss; from *moine* – moss or morass, and *mor* – big. Site of 'The Glenlivet' distillery.

Monadh a' Ghiuthais°
Pine tree moor; from *monadh* – moor, and *na ghiuthas* (genitive of *giuthas*) – pine tree. The moorland shoulder between Braeval and Blairwick (in Kirkmichael).

Nevie
(1680 Nevie) Sanctuary; from *neimhidh* – holy, sanctified. Chapel of Christ, which stood on the east bank of the Livet near the mouth of the Nevie Burn, and was the predecessor of the now vanished chapel in the Dounan cemetery, opposite Minmore.

Pole Inn
English, 19th century. 'Pole' is a common name for a crossroads or T-junction at which a marker pole may have been erected. The inn was established about 1842–4.

Poolwick*
(Locally 'Pollaweek') Buck's pool; from *poll a' bhuic* (genitive of *boc*) – roe-buck.

Quirn
(1761 Kirn, 1768 Keiurn; locally 'Keern') Possibly 'The Recess'; from *cearn* – recess

or corner; appropriate because of the long steep-sided course of the Slough Burn below Carn Ellick and its eastward ridge, Quirn Hill. The name is thus unlikely to derive from *carn* – cairn, although *guirean* – pimple, or *cirean* – crest, cock's comb, are possible. Probably the ancient name for the area, above which climbed the old track between Tomnavoulin and Kirkmichael that was abandoned after the knockandhu to Tomintoul road was built in 1823.

Refriesh (1636 Refrish, Refrush, 1794 Refruice) Hill-slope of thickets; from *ruigh* – hill-slope or cattle run, and *phreas* (genitive of *preas*) – thicket, bush. The suffix is unlikely to be *frith eas* – small water, while *fraoch* – heather, does not evolve into 'frish'. This upper end of The Baden (qv) was probably a shealing area until the 17th century.

Rhindu (1761 Rindow, 1817 Rindoo) Black point; from *roinn* point or headland, and *dhu* – black.

Riv 19th century. Cattle enclosure; from Scots *rieve* – animal pen. Croft opposite Demick. (See also Tomnarieve.)

Rosebrae English, late 19th century. Cottage near Easter Auchavaich.

Rosemount English, late 19th century. Near Daisy Cottage (qv).

Roughburn English, 19th century. House near Chapeltown to which the last miller at Achnascraw retired – previously Wester Achnascraw.

Scalan (1761 Scalin) Rough shelter; from *sgalan* – a temporary shelter formed by roofing a shallow trench with branches.

Scorranclach°
Small cliff of the stone; from *sgorran* (diminutive of *sgorr*) – small cliff or peak, and *clach* – stone. Hill west of Upper Clashnoir with rock outcrops and scattered boulders. (See also Glachan.)

Skyhouse
English, 19th century. A cottar house with yard and well on the skyline above Upper Clashnoir.

Slateford
English, 19th century. Site of crofts at the south side of Upper Clashnoir in 1761, but latterly a smithy. As the name suggests, the Allt Vattiern here flows through very slaty rock.

Slochd Burn°
Burn of the hollow; from *slochd* – pit or hollow. Runs into the Crombie just below Scalan.

Springlea
English, 20th century. Opposite Clashnoir Cottage.

Starryhillock
English, 19th century. 'Starr' is the Scots name for the bog rush, hence 'Rushyhillock'. Beside Auchnarrow, the site is now Woodside Cottage.

Strans*
(19th century) Small haugh; from *srathan* – small waterside haugh. A 'wee house in the heather' at Invernahaven, probably one of the cottar houses.

Strathavon
Valley of the River Avon; from *srath* – broad river valley (see Avon). Was also known historically as Strath Down.

Suie
(1638† Suiarthour) The glen, burn and farm take their name from Carn an t-Suidhe above them, which the 1638 reference identifies as 'Arthur's Seat', from *suidhe* – a seat. Despite being a recognised Scottish 'Arthur' site, neither local records nor traditions mention any

such association.

Thain
(1761 Thane) Unexplained. Although dating from the late 17th century this name is not obviously Gaelic, which has no 'th' sound ('t' aspirated is written 'th' but sounds as 'h'). It may be the degraded form of a Gaelic source such as *taine* – thin-ness (pronounced 'tane'), or (all with initial sound 'tye') *teanga* – tongue (of land), *teann* – tight, *teine* – fire, *tighearn* – lord, or *tinn* – chain, but nothing has been found to suggest which it may be.

Timberford
English 18th century. (1761 Timber-foord) This former croft on the Allt na Fanich, near Belachknockan, lies on the 'Timber Road', the route by which timber from the forests of Abernethy was transported down to Keith and beyond. Between Kirkmichael and Lettoch, the 'Timber Road' was also known as the 'Funeral Road'.

Tom a' Voan°
Knoll of the moss; from *tom* – knoll, and *mhoine* (genitive of *moine*) – a moss, but explained locally as 'knoll of the huts', from *bhothan* (genitive plural of *both*) – hut. This probably arose because the whole area had been summer shealing ground until the Auchavaichs were established in the 17th century and involved only a small change of inflection in the orginal name. Corrunich above West Auchavaich was still the Tomnalienan shealing area in the mid 18th century.

Tombae
Birch hill; from *beithe* – birch tree. Held in the mid 16th century by George

Gordon of Tombae, illegitimate brother of John Gordon of Cluny. (See also Achdregny and Achnascraw.)

Tombreck° (1761 Tambreck) Speckled knoll; from *tom* – hillock, and *breac* – speckled or piebald. Former croft beside Lettoch.

Tom Cruinn° Round hill; from *cruinn* – round. A hill west of Lettoch. (See also Glachan.)

Tomoriough° See Tomnarieve

Tomnalienan (1680 Tomnalinan, 1738 Tominlinean, 1750 Tomnalienan) knoll of the meadows; from *leana* – meadow, plural *leanan*. Although *lion* – flax is a possibility, flax-growing was not introduced into Upper Banffshire until the 1750s.

Tomnarieve* (1748 Tominrea, 1822 Tomoriough, 1830 Tomnarive) The present form of the name suggests 'hill of the enclosure', in a Gaelic/Scots hybrid of *tom na* – hill of, with Scots *rieve* – cattle enclosure. However, the older versions show that it was originally 'greyish little hillock', from *toman* – little hillock, and *riabhach* – brindled, grizzled. The change in name occurred between 1823 and 1830.

Tomnavoulin (1680 Tomnavillen) Hillock of the mill; from *tom na mhuilinn* (genitive of *muileann*) – mill.

Tom Trumper° Trumpeter Hill; from *trombair* – trumpeter. Phonetically, this is the only likely source of the name, but local tradition gives no explanation for its origin. Overlooks Scalan from the south west.

Tordhu* Black hill; from *tor* – hill, and *dhu* – black. Former croft just east of Upper

Auchnarrow, now vanished. This is also the name of the hill above Achbreck.

Tullich   (1768 Tulloch of Tombae) Knoll; from *tulach*. Possibly refers to the summit knoll of Carn Tullich.

Vatich Burn   'Tufted Burn'; from *badach* – abounding in tufts (of reeds or sedge). It drains the Fae Vatich (qv) and joins the Crombie opposite East Auchavaich.

Wester Scalan   See Scalan. Abandoned farm on the west bank of the Crombie near Clash of Scalan.

Westerton   West Auchavaich. The Westerton above Tomnavoulin was formerly Wester Corries (of Tomnavoulin).

Whitefolds   English 19th century. A farm between Achdregny and Cordregny.

Woodend   English 20th century. Greystone on 1957 O.S. map. At the roadside between the Kirkie and the Clashnoirs.

Woodside Cottage   English 19th century. There are two houses of this name – one at the back of Tom a' Voan and the other at Auchnarrow (see Starryhillock).

For further reading:

A. Watson & E. Allan *The Place Names of Upper Deeside,* 1984

W. J. Watson *Place Names of Ross & Cromarty,* 1904 (reprinted 1971)
  Celtic Place-names of Scotland, 1926 (reprinted 1986)

W. F. H. Nicolaisen *Scottish Place-Names,* Batsford 1976 (paperback 1986)

J. Macdonald *Place Names in Strathbogie,* 1891
  Place Names of West Aberdeenshire, 1899

W. Alexander *Place Names of Aberdeenshire,* 1952

18

.

A Brief History of the Braes

.

Alasdair Roberts

The briefest history of the Braes of Glenlivet can be given in the number of people who lived there. Records began for Inveravon (Ballindalloch to Scalan) with an estimated 2464 in 1755. The population dropped after a series of poor 18th century harvests, and again briefly at the end of the whisky smuggling era, but the general trend was upwards to the middle of the 19th century. There followed a slow and then rapid decline, the start of the last phase coinciding with these Tales. Glenlivet was not affected by the Highland Clearances, which displaced families for sheep, nor was Banffshire one of the distressed Crofting Counties which required legislation to keep people on the land. The Dukes of Gordon were good landlords, and on their estates (which stretched as far west as Lochaber) eviction was almost unknown. Left to itself, the population of Inveravon parish reached a peak of 2714 men, women and children in 1851, about a third of them living in the Braes of Glenlivet. There were still 500 beyond Knock-andhu at the outbreak of the First World War, and the Braes retained an ageing population of 260 in 1931 – the year when Isobel Grant left the area. Only about eighty people live there now.

Patches of soil in Glenlivet have been cultivated since the Picts, whose traces remain in 'Druidical temples' at Nevie and Deskie. Most of the ground has always been pasture, however. Like much of the Highlands, this was cattle country, and herds were driven south to Crieff and Falkirk by a drove road which started at Scalan. Cattle were the cause of an 18th-century conflict which changed the boundary between Banffshire and Aberdeenshire. Old men testified to changes in the flow of mountain streams in order to settle the landlord rights of Forbes and Gordon. This dispute over the Faevait shealing grounds was caused by Corgarff families settling on land made fertile by cattle which the young people of Strathavon and Strathdon had minded from summer bothies. Shealing was partly about keeping animals away from crops, because fields lacked dykes or fences. Perhaps the Braes of Glenlivet were nothing more than shealing land, until people pressed in during the 18th century?

There is very little on record about earlier centuries. The Earl of Argyll's invading army was driven back at Glenlivet in 1594, but the battle's other names of Alltachoileachan and Benrinnes show how vaguely it was remembered. Half a century later the Marquis of Huntly was captured at Delnabo (the field of the cattle, near modern Tomintoul) and taken to Edinburgh, where this chief of the Gordons was executed as a royalist. His royal master Charles I shared the same fate in the same year of 1649. So much for links with national history. Local history is glimpsed through the cattle thief Seamus an Tuim, who escaped from Edinburgh Castle later in the century. He lulled a Grant neighbour into thinking their feud was over by accepting his hospitality, and then his company on the final stage of the journey home: 'They had not gone far when the barbarian drew his sword and slew both the father and son; and having cut off their heads, wrapped them in a corner of his plaid, returned to Tomnavoulin, threw them reeking with blood into the lap of Mrs Grant and then bade her goodnight.'

This brings us deep into the Braes, because Scalan was

where Tomnavoulin shealed cattle. The records of the Scalan seminary are a useful source of information on everyday life at a time when hardly anyone else there could write, but they should not always be taken as gospel. Clergymen liked to dramatise their isolation when writing to Paris and Rome. The very presence of Scalan, training boys to become priests against the laws of Scotland, implied that the Braes were a hidden place at the world's end. In a sense they were. The first priest who lived there fled to the limits of Gordon territory after the Jacobite Rising of 1715. The bishop who erected the building which survives explained that the name came from 'sgailean', or shelters for hunters. And the seminary, with its back to the hills, was reached by a track through the great morass of the Vatich peat bog.

That adds to the feeling of desolation, but peat was also important for settlement. A minister of the time complained that with the moss outside Huntly exhausted, his people were forced to bring in coal from the coast. Despite the clergy view from Scalan, there was already a settled population when the students moved in. In the 17th century 'tacksmen' of the gentry class were paying rent for Braes holdings when Refriesh was a corn mill to Achnarrow and Clashnoir. Lettoch had been let to the Gordons of Minmore for generations. Achnascraw was a farm three hundred years before Chapeltown came into existence. The Duke of Gordon's factor was actually living at Demickmore, draining and improving the land, when Scalan opened in 1716. Nevertheless there was something in the nature of a Faevait situation in the Braes, for here, as on Donside, cattle were threatening corn. The Strathavon farm of Glenconglass used the land above Culraggie burn for shealing, and their herd grazed 'within pistol shot' of Clashnoir until the Duke's factor established that the area belonged to the Gordons.

It was from Clashnoir that important letters were sent to Rome in 1733 after one of the annual clergy meetings at Scalan, and what was then called Bochel Hall also had church connections. The priest who lived there marched to Derby with the men of Glenlivet, and was wounded at Culloden while attending them. Soon after the battle his house was burned to the ground, and Cumberland's men went on to do the same at Scalan. But John Gordon of Glenbucket had such a notorious reputation for forcing men out in Jacobite risings that Glenlivet did not suffer much after the final one. The Duke had stayed aloof from the 'wicked rebellion', and hardly any Gordon tenants were transported to the colonies. None was executed. Books and altar vestments were burned, but damage to buildings was hardly serious because turf 'black houses' could easily be restored: small ones went up in a day.

Heather-thatched dwellings could be elaborate, however, with several rooms and box-bed compartments. There had always been a few superior buildings in the Braes, and 'white' houses of stone and lime came in with the new Scalan of 1767. Scarcely half a dozen buildings had stone chimneys at the end of the century, however. Stone for houses came from field-gatherings, not quarries, as cultivation increased. One of the finest fermtouns belonged to the McPhersons of Tomnalienan, whose fifty acres of corn land were renowned. Commenting on the richer, deeper soil in the upper part of his parish, Ballindalloch's minister observed: 'There is in the head of Glenlivet an excellent marl-pit and the farm of Tomalinan, beside whose land the marl-pit is, lies mostly on a rock of limestone.' Clay and lime meant good farm land, and the Belno, or new town of Tomnalienan brought further acres under the plough. Gordon estate papers show other 'new lands' being taken in for arable beside the Crombie.

The unexpected death of the last Catholic Duke of Gordon in 1728 scarcely affected the Braes, although for a while some Catholic fathers went down to Ballindalloch to have their oldest sons (only) baptised. The Duchess made no objection to the seminary, for Scalan was valued as an experimental farm. In the age of agricultural improvement, priests with an excellent library to hand were quick to learn new ways. Archibald Grant of Monymusk was Scotland's leading improver, and in its last phase Scalan bought meal from the

Leslies of Fetternear, beside Monymusk. The Scalan community was never self-sufficient, nor should it have been since education was the point of the exercise – although there were complaints about the boys spending too much time on outdoor work in summer. This included the preparation of peat for winter. School rules tried to protect these would-be priests from outside influences, but there were many visitors: Scalan employed smiths, wrights, tailors and other craftsmen as well as day labourers paid for 'mowing the grass park and putting the irons of the scythes in order.'

Seminary land was drained as fields were enclosed and fertilised. Neighbours took note, and some followed: much later there were estate rules to enforce crop rotation. The Scalan dykes which protected growing crops from animals can still be seen. Lime was obtained by breaking stones for the kiln beside the approach road. The Scalan account book itemised oats, bere, barley, malt and hops (for ale) under Corn – some of it home-grown but most bought in. Towards the end of the century the seminary increased its flock, but 'the sheep which eat up men' never afflicted Glenlivet. One curious item in the Scalan accounts touches on two kinds of improvement: 'The hacket quoy died on the clover this day.' Perhaps clover, a great novelty when it was introduced to enrich the soil, was too rich for this white-faced heifer. Its all-black forebears had been driven to the hill without winter feed, but the entry shows that the clergy and their farm managers were into cross-breeding early.

The natives of the Braes are still silent in the 1780s, and it is from Scalan records that we hear of extremes of climate which affected everybody: 'The snow is so deep that there is scarcely a possibility of travelling between towns. The people are only drinking down sorrow and, with the whisky bottle, banishing away the melancholy thoughts of bad times.' New Year 1784 came in without mercy: 'Most desperate days. A furious easterly wind laid all level; several houses were overturned; no less than twelve stacks of corn driven God knows where; the poor people prodding the snow with poles for their sheep buried fifteen to twenty feet below.' Wet summers and poor harvests were so frequent that there was rejoicing in 1788 when, for the first time in seven years, crops were in by October. Families began to move out, looking for work elsewhere. Abbé MacPherson recalled poor harvests leading to death from starvation. In the summer of 1741 people bled cattle every second day for their own nourishment.

Cattle were also involved in the growing of corn, as a visiting tailor James Phillips learned from his clients – a first source of evidence from local people: 'Fancy eight or ten strong oxen drawing a wooden plough with scarcely so much iron about it as would form the beam of a plough of the present day. These oxen were of the Highland breed, shaggy brutes with tremendous horns.' One farmer being measured for a suit recalled 'a man following the plough without a stocking or shoe on his feet, and in asking him if his feet were cold to receive the following reply that they were "some caul till he got them into the last furrow".' People helped each other in the spirit of runrig, although fields were allocated to individual tenants long before the end of the century: 'Everyone, almost, had a plough though very many of them wanted the harness. It was told to me by an old gentleman still living in the Braes that there were seven families living in the farm which he occupies at present and they all had ploughs, but he never saw them all yoked at one time. The one who chanced to be up earliest generally took the liberty of supplying himself with his neighbour's harness. Yet they all got on very agreeably and very well.'

In 1799, with the government now willing to forget the Jacobite past, Scalan was abandoned for a larger college beside Fetternear. Other changes marked out the 1790s as the end of an era. Oats now grew in places where there had been grass from the beginning of time, but there were still scarcely a thousand acres under the plough. Much draining remained to be done, but a significant pause in agricultural improvement now followed. Partly this was because Britain went to war with

France over a twenty-year period, and the Glenlivet estate contributed a full share of men for the Gordon Highlanders. But veterans who returned when peace was signed in 1815 encountered a new type of economic activity. Scotland's growing cities were generating demand for another Highland product (beyond cattle). Just as Aberdeen has been transformed by the North Sea Oil boom in our time, so a large part of north-east Scotland was altered by what may fairly be called the Glenlivet Whisky boom.

Although 'usquebaugh' was ancient, the rise of whisky-making for sale to outsiders began in the 1780s. Braes people 'drinking down sorrow' must have found it difficult to grow enough barley for house whisky, and can hardly have managed to brew ale during bad harvests which included a 'pease-bread year' of scarcely any corn. Once an industry developed and markets were obtained, however, barley was brought up from the fertile Laigh of Moray. By the 19th century's opening decade every house had its still – two hundred have been estimated for Glenlivet, most of them in the Braes. Whisky-making became such a common activity that people found it hard to believe they were breaking the law as it changed by stages. Westminster introduced the licensing of stills in 1786 and prohibited those of less than 500 gallons in 1814. A desperate last period of conflict with the law followed the 1824 Excise Act. It was introduced to Parliament by the Duke of Gordon and brought the small still era to an end within ten years. George Smith of Upper Drummin was only producing fifty gallons a week when he decided to defy local opinion (with two pistols as his constant companions) and build the legal distillery whose successor flourishes at Minmore.

Simple to set up, the domestic still was easy to move to a hillside bothy. The copper cooling tube (or 'yowie wi' the crookit horn') was bought with earnings from Perthshire harvests – from 'tin'-making tinkers – to make the pure Glenlivet malt which gentlemen craved in Edinburgh. Raw materials counted for something, but the actual water of life varied a good deal. Astonishingly pure in the Slochd above

Scalan, it ranged from the iron of Fuerandearg's red well to the pot-furring lime of Eskemulloch. Blyeside farms produced the best whisky, and the modern distillery at Chapeltown gets its water from Ladderfoot. Four-gallon barrels and hardy ponies to carry them, four at a time, were part of the investment. City merchants came out to meet columns of men whom the law had turned into smugglers. Braes men went south to Brechin, east to Aberdeen, and occasionally north down Glenrinnes for the coastal trade. More than its ingredients, or the patient skills of those who handled malt and mash, it was the strategic position of Glenlivet which gave it a name for Highland whisky in general.

The smuggling era generated its own tales of the Braes of Glenlivet – in particular a fatally popular song by John Milne o' Livet's Glen, a Stonehaven cobbler who lived with his wife's people at Demick. The sheets sold so well at feeing markets that they became the subject of official complaint. Sung to the tune of 'Johnny Cope', Milne's sixty-four-verse epic described a campaign by the excise officers against Glen Nochty, over the Ladder, whose bothies were defended by bolder spirits from the Braes:

> Glen Noughty lads they staid at hame,
> For fear that they should get the blame,
> But Glenlivet men they thought no shame
> For to keep their ground in the morning.
>
> The Preventive commander said, We'll retire,
> We cannot longer stand their fire,
> Though it be sore against my desire,
> To leave their glens in the morning.
>
> You are the lads we dare not mock,
> We find them firm like any rock,
> So they ran like a fugie cock,
> And left their glens in the morning.

The gaugers returned with military support, but these soldiers did not care for their assignment. Again information comes from the tailor who wrote it all down:

One day the preventives were marching up a hill with the intention of capturing some smugglers who were situated at the brow of it. They commenced to hurl down stones upon the preventives who, seeing this, shouted loudly to the soldiers to come on. They were taking it quite easy a good distance in the rear. They advanced, however, to the bottom of the hill. The smugglers on seeing this desisted, but the officer in command shouted in Gaelic to throw down more. The smugglers at once obeyed, and with such effect that the preventives beat a hasty retreat.

The only real prosperity that the people of the Braes ever knew came to an end in the 1830s. There was a garrison at Corgarff castle for the first time since the military road had been pushed through to Spey, and Glenlivet men were taken as prisoners to Perth. Still more to the point, the Duke made it clear that he was serious about evicting tenants who broke the law – a later case near Huntly won public sympathy but no reprieve. Many consignments of whisky were seized, and when the smugglers did win through the dealers were liable to cheat them. Tombae's priest was a witness to this: 'Your nephew Paul Grant Achdregnie continued for the first two or three years after I came to Glenlivet to drive the staple commodity of the country to Strathmore. He met with many serious losses in that quarter and had debts which he never received. Soon after he abandoned that abominable traffic of driving the mountain dew, took his farm and married.' A loan was obtained through this man of the cloth, and the Grants became upright members of his congregation. The minister's Statistical Account of 1836, by way of contrast, lacked something in Christian charity:

> The energetic measures taken by Government for the suppression of smuggling have proved eminently successful. The male population, instead of prowling over the country in search of a market for their whisky and being constantly on the watch to elude the eye of excise officers, are now happily and successfully employed in the cultivation of farms or in prosecuting handicrafts, while the females, who were in the

habit of spending no small portion of their time, by night as well as by day, in the bothy – a prey to the licentious and immoral – are now more safely and suitably employed. Under the guidance of a faithful and judicious clergyman in the full enjoyment of the status and emoluments of a parish minister, it might be hoped that, under the Divine blessing, the whole inhabitants of Glenlivet would gradually be improved.

Leaving aside the fact that the Rev. Asher's father was himself a licensed distiller, these observations seem harsh. To turn from smuggling to cultivation or handicrafts was not easy. Some men took up driving cattle to England, but that ancient activity was already in decline and the railways finished it off. Young men began to leave permanently in search of work – farming in the colonies or whatever they could get in the cities, home or abroad. Reformed smugglers found a welcome in the police. But how 'safely and suitably employed' could the women be who stayed behind? With memories of 'bothy nichts', and sometimes children as more tangible souvenirs, they had little chance of marriage with all the men away.

The minister was also wrong to suggest that Catholic clergy failed to give moral leadership, although there was certainly a gap after the last priest left Scalan in 1807. A Benedictine of Fort Augustus admitted as much, before going on to describe the 1829 changes at Chapeltown:

The population of the higher part was subjected to a great inconvenience for receiving instruction and attending the duties of their religion. There was no bridge over the Livet, and all the good folks from the Braes – the womenkind at least – walked barefoot till they crossed the river. To remedy this evil Abbé Paul MacPherson set about erecting a new chapel and schools. Having obtained from the Duke of Gordon, for whom he had done some service in Rome, a central spot of ground, he raised upon it a neat and commodious chapel seated for about three hundred persons and a dwelling-house for the clergyman, together with good farm buildings. He not only erected these but supplied them with all necessary vestments and [altar] furniture, receiving no assistance from any quarter but what the people of the country gave him in the carriage of materials. He also improved the piece of ground attached to the chapel, a part of which was laid out as a cemetery.

The third phase of this history may be linked, through Chapeltown, with what planners call 'infrastructure' but is more happily conveyed in verse. The achievements of the military engineer George Wade, bringing roads to the Highlands, have been celebrated in a well known couplet:

> If you'd seen these roads before they were made,
> You'd hold up your hands and bless General Wade.

This is echoed by a less well known couplet from the Braes of Glenlivet:

> If you'd seen these roads before there were any,
> You'd hold up your hands and bless Mr Glennie.

Mr James Glennie ('Father' was not yet used by Scottish priests) came to Chapeltown in 1846. He gave the landlord and his factor no peace until a metalled road was brought into the heart of the Braes.

The first road from lower Inveravon was built by the Grants of Ballindalloch, joining the Duke of Gordon's road from Dufftown to his model village of Tomintoul which was founded for linen-making in 1776. Several years passed before houses appeared there, and with linen failing throughout Scotland the village only got going in the following century. It became the market for Braes stock taken by Lettoch and Inchnacape. A toll road ran through Tomintoul from Grantown-on-Spey to the south, but the Lecht was always dangerously steep. The 'county' road brought a post-chaise up Glenrinnes from Aberdeen by way of Keith, with a runner required to take mail three times a week on the final stage up Avonside to Tomintoul. There was no road for sprung vehicles in the direction of the Braes after Tomnavoulin, and people walked in if no packhorse or farm cart was available. Travellers from the south were just as likely to arrive by the 'Whisky Roadie'.

Bridges were vulnerable, and the Muckle Spate of 1829 damaged several. A new road from Achnarrow to Tomintoul was begun in 1824, but twelve years later a connection between Tomnavoulin and Achnarrow was still one of the 'improvements most wanted'. At a time when Mr Glennie's Chapeltown road was still to be constructed, it is curious to read in the Statistical Account of a proposed branch road from Tomnalienan to Tomintoul, and also another, 'if practicable', to Glenbucket and Strathdon by way of the Ladder. The local habit of blaming economic problems on poor roads can also be expressed in verse. The following lines by the Rev. Robert Calder of Achbreck concern the difficulty of obtaining a new tenant:

> At length, frae laicher doon the shire,
> A man, who wanted to be higher,
> Cam' up the vacant farm to see,
> An' maybe for't an offerer be.
> The farm the stranger steppit owre,
> An' roun about him keen did glower,
> An' a' the points, both good an' ill,
> His e'e took in wi' practised skill.
>
> And then says he, 'The place, I find,
> Is nae ill-suited to my mind;
> The soil is good to be sae high,
> An' fairly to the sun does lie,
> An' on that pasture on the moor
> Baith sheep and stirks wad thrive, I'm sure;
> But I maun say I think it odd
> That there is nae a better road,
> In fact that there's no road ava'
> On which to cart the corn awa'.'

The improvement of farm land was resumed after the collapse of whisky, with waste ground being turned into arable at the rate of a hundred acres a year in the mid-century. Crofters were involved at the margin. When the ducal line came to an end the Gordon inheritance passed to the first Duke of

Richmond and Gordon. He met formally with tenants in 1842 to agree new leases at Glenfiddoch. There were new rules attached, among them the adoption of a five-shift rotation which included turnips. The large farms of lower Glenlivet set an example in the liming of fields and crop husbandry: George Smith was able to supply most of his distillery from the Minmore farm. Oats were the staple, as ever, with barley or bere sown after the fallow year of grass (for hay). Wheat only grew well in the lower district, however, and by the time Phillips was writing things down the system had failed – in the opinion (surprisingly 'green') of those who tried to apply it:

> The five-shift system will not do in the Braes of Glenlivet. The soil is naturally cold, and in many parts of no great depth. For turnips it requires about four hundredweight of artificial manure, over and above the home manures. The artificial manures generally used are stimulants and simply force up a crop, the natural consequence being that the soil is getting shallower every year. In some farms where seven or eight years ago the plough could run a hundred or two hundred yards without coming in contact with a single stone, it is now grating on the bottom and coming in contact with earth-fast stones.

Natural resources were also being used up in another way. The Vatich peat moss which once sheltered Scalan had by now been 'casten' over three times in layers of eight to ten feet. With 120,000 barrowfuls a year being taken out in the 1870s, the area's main source of fuel was almost exhausted.

Most Braes tenants could not afford artificial fertilisers and believed that their fields needed more time under grass to recover – a move back towards pastoral farming. Things came to a head in a period of general agricultural depression when the landlord responded to written complaint:

> I have received the memorial from the Braes of Glenlivet tenants asking for a reduction of rent. It is most gratifying for me to know that your forefathers have been tenants under my family for generations, but I did not anticipate that I should be asked to make a reduction of rent on the ground that 1877 was a bad season. When the accounts were closed in August of that

year there was not a single penny of arrear, and whilst I readily admit that this could not have been the case if you had not been industrious I cannot but take it as proof that the rents had been adjusted on the principle of 'live and let live'. I am sure that you would not desire that you should derive all the benefits of good years and that I should bear the loss in less prosperous times. The subject was constantly under my attention when in the north this autumn and the state of your crops was brought fully before me at the end of October. I arranged in consequence that the collection of rents should be postponed for three months.

The Napier Commission toured Scotland in 1883 gathering evidence on crofting. Banffshire was not involved, but a writer in the *North British Agriculturalist* offered an East Highland view which justified the Duke's 'live and let live' – at least for small holdings:

Where people have planted themselves down on the hillside, the rent is only the eighth part of a sovereign. Some of the crofts were made up of the outlying portions of arable farms where the land had been under the plough before. In that case a common rent is £2 for from 7 to 10 acres – sufficient to keep two cows and a stirk, or a cow, a calf and a pony. This is extremely cheap. The crofters seem content, and so they may. Many crofters in the same county who occupy land that was arable before they got it pay nearly three times as much rent as the Duke's small holders do.

Gordon tenants were allowed to keep three sheep for every pound rent, and crofters who 'planted' themselves beside the free pasture of the hills took full advantage – although the Rev. Asher, writing in 1836, reported the view of leading farmers that these 'stunted' hill sheep were hardly worth the trouble. He also contrasted the Aberdeen-Angus herd at Ballindalloch with 'cattle in general throughout the parish, bred without much attention to the selection of bulls or cows and kept in numbers quite disproportionate to the food, which is often unpalatable as well as scanty, and equally destitute of symmetry as of flesh'. A pedigree herd was nevertheless produced by

169

George Smith on the distillery farm at Minmore, and at Tombae the Rev. Charles Macdonald also won prizes for cattle.

Low rents and free hill pasture go far to explain why the Braes of Glenlivet held on to a considerable population until well into the present century, crofters being encouraged to settle on marginal land. The estate employed shepherds to keep the flocks on high ground, and this produced another kind of social benefit. The Shepherds' Ball which took place at the Mill of Achnascraw on 25th September, 1880, was organised by a committee drawn from Calier, Scalan, Bolletten, Braeval and Demickmore. The ball (seemingly a fairly new event) was run by a 'floormaster' called Macdonald. The sole – and heroic – musician was a Watt from Refriesh on fiddle and bagpipes. Shepherds came from as far as Suie and Corgarff, and 'the youth and beauty of the Braes of Glenlivet turned out in such large numbers that the large room was perfectly crowded. During the night refreshments were distributed with a liberal hand, while songs and toasts frequently relieved the dancers.'

A linked item in the *Banffshire Journal* reported on more serious activities which suggested that the father of another fiddler-piper was not at the ball: 'The weather during the week has not been so favourable for harvest operations as would be wished. A considerable quantity has however been got into the stackyard in good order, some having even finished, among them Mr G. Grant, Bochel.' The Mill of Achnascraw was where James Phillips plied his trade as tailor, so it is worth mentioning a rather different social event, the Glenlivet Volunteer Ball, which was held in January at Minmore. Private Phillips and Private Lamb from Scalan went down to offer themselves as partners to ladies of the Braes like Miss Macpherson, Tomnalienan, and Miss Nellie Gordon, Lettoch. Most of the eighty who attended were from Lower Glenlivet, however. Music on this occasion was provided by four fiddles, a flute and a cornet. The ballroom, normally a granary, was decorated with evergreens, roses and badges of other Volunteer units. A banner with 'Let Glenlivet Flourish!'

referred to the local whisky as well as the area.

On that convivial note, we close.